THE
BROKEN

TAINTED TRAIL

A. L. FRANCES

Ruby Rose Publishing

Amazon PAPERBACK
© Copyright 2020
A.L Frances

The right of A.L Frances to be identified as author of this work has been asserted
by her in accordance with the Copyright, Designs and Patents Act 1988.

A CIP catalogue record for this title is available from the British Library.

ISBN 978-0-9601051-1-3

This is a work of fiction. Names, characters, businesses, places,
events, locales, and incidents are either the products of the author's
imagination or used in a fictitious manner. Any resemblance to actual
persons, living or dead, or actual events is purely coincidental.

Amazon is an imprint of Ruby Rose Publishing House.
www.RubyRosePublishingHouse.com

First Published in 2020
Amazon
Printed & Bound in Great Britain

AUTHOR'S NOTE

My purpose for writing the series of *The Broken* novels extends above and beyond just wanting to write a gripping close to home story.

On occasions, I've picked up books and been unable to visualise what the writer has so beautifully written for me. Then, when I've found a book I've loved and read it to the end, the sense of achievement is immeasurable. I believe everyone should embrace this emotion when they read.

My desire is for you to feel just as wonderful when you reach the end of this novel, as I've written this wholeheartedly for you!

DEDICATION

I wrote this for you...

A. L. Frances

CONTENTS

PROLOGUE

How easy is it to go from having everything you have ever wanted, to having nothing? One day you wake up and you have it all, and then, in the very same twenty-four-hours, you lose everything in more ways than one. You lose your freedom, your family, your career, your sanity, your reason for living, your very existence, everything! It doesn't matter how big or small the loss is, it's gone, with no likelihood of returning any time soon. That said, how would you feel...? Before you answer, consider this: you cannot escape fate, there's no way of getting around it – your final destination can rarely be changed, your soul has signed a lifelong contract, whether you accept this path or not.

You see, your journey into life truly begins to unfold as you grow. The premeditated pathway, which has been carefully constructed and perfectly aligned for you, can sometimes have a freakishly unconventional way of presenting you with challenges. Here's the thing: the cards which you are dealt can ensure that you, the lucky recipient, receive all your wishes and hearts desires, experiencing the great satisfaction of all that this blessing has to offer. A sense of joy, happiness, laughter and love. But, hang on a minute – these are the same cards that can, by a twist of fate, lead you, the unlucky recipient, to soul-destroying and unfortunate circumstances. You may believe these negative and sometimes traumatic moments in your life are completely out of your control – but are they? Or do you, without knowing, actually build the path and welcome them in...?

Our unlucky protagonist from the first instalment of *The Broken* suffers the brutal death of his wife due to a horrific event that he witnesses but is unable to prevent. It becomes apparent years later that this murderous unresolved incident stems from a tangled web of deceitful, impure intentions. To then lose his only child to the same calculated and cruel entity that is connected to the death of his wife is the ultimate blow.

And if that isn't bad enough, now he's the main focus of an investigation into the disappearance of his daughter. The authorities have now also decided to reopen the case regarding the death of his wife, a death which they themselves initially wrote off as an unfortunate accident. They're now suggesting that this is, in fact, a potential murder case, a crime which they're also trying to pin on this broken man. It will be tricky for him to prove his innocence as it is reliant on his daughter somehow appearing alive and well, but it isn't impossible. He knows she isn't dead. Her body is still very much alive. It's her soul that has been captured and cursed. Now, the question is, what do you think you would do?

Your current situation is very isolated. You have support from no one. There isn't one person in the world that believes a single word you're saying. Everyone has turned their back on you – the only reason you haven't been sectioned is that no one cares enough to protect you. Your friends and family are treating you as though the offences the authorities are alleging you have committed are the truth. They all believe you perpetrated such awful crimes and killed the people you not only loved but lived for. And add to that mental anguish, the claim that it is you who disposed of your own child's body, due to the fact that its whereabouts to date remain unknown. You're left with nothing and no one. You're being hissed at in the street and physically abused each time you try to defend your word, and now, the next twisted challenge life has presented you with, which you face alone, is that there is only one way for you to clear your name, seemingly one, almost impossible, way… You must hunt down the evil entity who ruined your life and kill it. Not only this, you somehow have to reveal its true intentions to the world and pray that you can save your daughter's soul and free her from the evil shackles she's been cunningly strapped into in the process. It won't be easy and all you have available to you is hope in your heart and a trail that's almost freezing cold. Are you feeling brave enough yet? Bearing all of this in mind, which path do you believe you would you choose:

Live and accept the hands of fate by spending the rest of your life in prison for crimes you didn't commit?

Begin the hunt with the faith that you can not only clear your tainted name but at the same time free your daughter from the evil that possesses her soul?

Choose death. After all, why help the world that turned its back on you? Align your own fate and give your soul to the afterlife. Take the secrets of this cruel sadistic entity's true catastrophic intentions to the deathly grave with you.

Well, here's how one man faced that exact dilemma, and the question is, what path will Matthew Honey select...?

CHAPTER ONE

Replay...

The Honey residence stands tall on the dark beachfront. The garden is overgrown and neglected. Inside, the entrance is completely unrecognizable. A family picture that was once proudly displayed in the doorway now lies face up on the floor, the glass is shattered. In the photo, Matthew, Lauren and Evelyn Jade Honey stand side by side with radiant smiles, glowing features. They appear to be the perfect happy family unit.

The temperature is sub-zero and a strong, sinister vibration trembles throughout the building. Resembling a horrific murder scene, this house is no longer a home. The walls showcase where gaping holes have been whacked through them. Embedded deep with grime and stained with huge splatters of blood, these same once bright walls that held happiness within this household now possess secrets that would make an innocent and playful soul curl up and beg for mercy. The tall, dark, intimidating looking walls give away the realities of the events which have taken place inside this once loved family home. It's clear to see that sickening and terrible things have happened here, things that could scar a mind forever.

Standing alone in the day room is a huge, eccentric golden frame, the remains of a once beautiful mirror. This previously treasured décor item has nothing but tiny shards of glass left hanging around the edges. Sitting directly in front of it, next to the huge window, is a dark wooden rocking chair. The seat is empty and worn.

Continuing the theme, the thick curtains, which are closed tight, were no doubt expensive, but their golden colour now barely shows through the filth. Suddenly, the wooden rocking chair begins to rock unaided, creaking as it moves back and forth in time with the unnerving vibration which continually manifests throughout the house.

Alongside this unannounced energy, a powerful stench is taking ownership of the room. It is so vile it would turn your insides. If this wasn't bad enough, the carpet throughout the dayroom is coated with matted hair, dust balls and dead insects – even Mother Nature's tiny creatures cannot tolerate this foul environment. Knotted deep within the mess are layer upon layer of skin-piercing shards of glass, most of which is stained with the same dried blood.

Standing within the shadows of the hallway is a spiral staircase that leads to the darker and higher points of this unloved house. Coated with thick smears of the same blood, it's certainly not a stairway that you would want to walk up alone. It's almost impossible to process how this formerly happy family home, which was filled with laughter and love, has now become the complete opposite. It's been tainted by evil and remains quiet and cold, a real-life house of horrors.

And yet this house is not, in fact, empty. The sound of girly, slightly out-of-tune singing is coming from one of the rooms upstairs. It gradually echoes throughout the building, the tone at odds with the heavy atmosphere. The soundwaves of the melody are sweet and angelic, with a detectable hint of happiness. The voice, an innocent female voice, is familiar and known.

Upstairs, the hallway is dark and eerie. All the doors are closed; all, that is, except for one. The office door is wide open. All the books have been thrown on the floor and the wooden bookcase in which they were once proudly showcased has been smashed to pieces. The dark oak wooden desk, positioned in the centre of the room, remains strong and is without a single scratch. Standing on top of the desk, also untouched, is a computer. The computer is switched on and prerecorded footage is playing on the monitor. The volume is turned up to the maximum. The footage is of Evelyn Jade Honey. It's replaying the morning of the seventh of July on a loop. The date when Matthew Honey last saw his daughter. Looking her usual radiant and innocent self, Eve is sat at the desk in her bedroom, her violin on her bed. Through the computer speakers you can hear her distorted voice singing along to pop music on the radio as she writes an entry in her red leather diary.

As the footage continues to play, a sudden rustling sound comes from inside the office, accompanied by a groan. Behind the open door, sprawled out on the floor with a litre bottle of vodka in his hand, wearing faded black ripped jeans with a grey t-shirt that's never seen soap and is drenched with blood, lies Matthew Honey, a broken man. Beaten within an inch of his life, his appearance is devastating – his eyes are deep purple, his nose inflamed and broken, his body covered in lacerations and bruises. This once strong family man who had everything is now a fraction of the man he was. He has passed out from the amount of alcohol he's consumed. Just above his head, hidden amongst all the books, mess and sharp shards of wood, is his black 9-mm pistol and it's loaded.

Matthew moans out loud in agony as he wakes. He releases his grip on the bottle of vodka and pulls out his mobile phone, which is vibrating in his pocket. The screen is completely smashed and is flashing like a strobe light. It's a call from an undisclosed number. Before he has time to press the accept button, the caller hangs up. His arms feel heavy. He drops them to the floor with a huge sigh as he reaches for his broken ribcage to support himself as he sits up. Achieving this with an immense amount of discomfort and difficulty, he looks over at the computer and sees the footage of Evelyn Jade playing. Instantly, tears begin uncontrollably welling in his bruised and swollen eye sockets. As the drops of sorrow descend his broken features, his phone begins to ring again. Reaching over and grumbling out in pain, Matthew manages to grab it and answers with a husky and dry voice, "Ello".

"Mr Honey, it's Kelly. Where are you?"

"Go away."

"Mr Honey, this is serious. If you don't get to Lymington Police Station in the next hour, a warrant is going to be issued for your arrest."

"Kelly, you seem to think I care. Why's that?" The long silence indicates that she doesn't know what to say next. "My point exactly. Goodbye, Kelly."

But before he puts the phone down, she speaks once more. "Mr Honey – please, if you go to prison now for breaching your bail conditions, how will you prove your innocence?" There is a brief silence as Matthew processes her words. "You know Chief Inspector Lamont has been after you for months. Please, don't give him the satisfaction of not only bringing you in, but arresting you and locking you away." More silence. Kelly pleads one final time, "Mr Honey, listen, I believe something did happen to Evelyn Jade, and I believe that it wasn't you who did it. Please don't give up on yourself and your daughter."

"Wait – you... believe... me?"

"Yes."

"Why?"

"I'm a good judge of character. Also, I've been a criminal PA to Mr Johnson for many years now. Working at his law firm has allowed me to witness many things, Mr Honey, and I know a genuine honest man when I see one. Don't give up on your daughter. If you don't get to the bottom of it, who else will? Only you know the truth..."

With the footage of Evelyn Jade continuing to play in the background and the tears still falling down his face, Matthew feels a deep sense of comfort from this young woman's words. His head starts to spin from the shock. Falling back, Matthew drops the phone on the floor next to his ear. After he doesn't respond for a while, Kelly shouts, "*Mr Honey... Mr Honey...* Shall I tell Mr Johnson that you'll attend the station?"

Closing his eyes and breathing in deep, he hears Kelly's words vibrate through the speaker. Matthew picks the phone back up and replies, "Yes." He then instantly ends the call.

Matthew's thoughts race at a hundred miles per hour. He doesn't know what to think, feel or do. After all these months, this is the first person who has said, true or not, that they believe him. That they believe he didn't kill his daughter or wife. He's been constantly beaten for defending his word, verbally abused for not admitting what others believe to be true, and now, he has a single fragment, a tiny, speck-of-glitter-sized glimmer of hope, because someone believes not only in him, but in what he says. Lying back, utterly drained, Matthew peers at the mess just above his head. Seeing a shimmer from the pistol hiding in the midst of the chaos, he slowly reaches up and holds the destructive weapon in his hand.

"End it all... How easy would that be?"

With a crazed expression, no longer in control of his thoughts, Matthew places the pistol against his temple. He squeezes the trigger slightly with his forefinger. He breathes rapidly, the torturous and cruel side of his mind teasingly whispering words, goading him to do the unthinkable.

"Do it, Matthew... Do it... Pull the trigger... Do it... Now!!"

Tears stream from his eyes and mucus gushes uncontrollably from his nose. He squeezes the trigger that tiny bit tighter and tighter. Just as the bullet is about to release, Matthew throws the pistol across the room. He puts his head into his hands and sobs out loud. His mind continues its unkind ways, his internal voice persistently whispering destructive and cruel words.

"Pathetic. You're so weak. You couldn't save your family and now you can't do the one decent thing and kill yourself for your sins..."

Picking the bottle of vodka up from the floor, he throws it across the room and shouts, "Just shut up!"

The bottle hits the wall and smashes, its contents splashing everywhere. Sharp shards of glass from the bottle now coat the layers of filth on the ground. Screaming out in frustration as a red mist takes over his thoughts, Matthew stumbles up onto his feet. Gaining control of his balance, he begins throwing everything in his proximity around the room. His rage is short-lived and soon he runs out of breath. An immense sense of pain hits as the red mist abates and the reality of his physical broken state takes over. Falling to the floor, Matthew positions himself with his back against the desk, slightly curled over.

Emotionally and physically exhausted, he puts his head down and weeps. Blood trickles down his enflamed and wounded knuckles. As he tries to gather his thoughts, he whispers to himself, "Just stop, please, I beg you. I can't take it anymore, I'm tired."

As he regains control of his emotions, his blood pressure drops slowly and the adrenaline leaves his body. Matthew's head is throbbing. Wiping the moisture from his face, and once again holding his ribcage, he lifts himself up off the ground in agony, reaching for the office chair that he threw at the wall. Surprisingly, this is still in one piece. He slumps into the seat and stares at the looping footage of his daughter. She's so innocent and beautiful. So pure and sweet. She's exactly how he wants to remember her. Matthew whispers, "Evelyn Jade Honey, please – where are you?" As the tears begin anew, he takes a moment to embrace happier memories. They flash like a home movie in his mind. "I miss you so much, kidda."

Reaching inside his jeans pocket, Matthew grasps an item tightly in his hand. He kisses it then opens his palm. It's the heart-shaped locket, the hunter. Bringing it close to his chest, Matthew recalls the sweeter times this treasured piece of jewellery represents. When things were pure and untainted. But just as his heart begins to warm, he sees her! He sees the evil entity who has devoured his daughter's soul: Jezebel.

Instantly, the rage returns. Clenching his fists and grinding his teeth, he holds the tainted item by the chain. Bringing the dangling locket up to his face and looking the engraved angel straight in the eye, he says, "I don't care where you are. I will find you. I will find you and I will get my daughter back and clear my name. I'm coming for you, you evil bitch. You will not win."

He bangs his fists on the table for emphasis and then places the chain around his neck, tucking the locket under his grubby t-shirt. He picks up the pistol from across the room, places it down the back of his jeans and makes his way out of the office.

He storms into his dark unwelcoming bedroom. Kicking the debris and mess out of his path, he grabs his black leather jacket off the floor and slips it on carefully over his injuries, along with his black wool beanie hat. Looking into the free-standing cracked mirror, he pulls the hood up on his jacket, he won't be recognised as the Matthew Honey people once knew.

The image in the mirror is dark, gloomy and unnerving. Blood is splattered everywhere. He stares directly at his reflection. With his head low and his swollen features, Matthew looks intimidating – and that's how he wishes to be seen: like a guy you wouldn't want to bump into alone on a dark night. Content with his disguise, he makes his way downstairs.

Entering the kitchen, he tops up his alcohol levels by drinking the dregs of whiskey straight from a bottle on the countertop. He then searches the kitchen, the empty glass bottles clinking together as he rummages for one containing alcohol. He finds a small bottle of vodka, which he places in the hidden pocket on the inside of his jacket. Snatching his wallet from the black marble kitchen countertop, Matthew checks that his picture of Eve is in pride of place. He kisses the image before he closes the wallet and puts it into his jeans pocket. Ready to get his act together, Matthew leaves the house to complete his first challenge of the day: adhering to his monthly bail condition and reporting to Lymington Police Station.

CHAPTER TWO

The Truth Hurts

Matthew parks just over half a mile away from the police station – after all, he wouldn't want to risk being arrested for driving under the influence. He takes a swig of vodka straight from the bottle then throws it into the dirty cream leather glove compartment. Reaching under the driver's seat, he grabs the pistol from where he has hidden it and throws this into the glove compartment, too. It clinks loudly against the glass of the bottle. As he looks into the compartment to check that the bottle hasn't smashed, he notices a brown leather-coated book tucked away at the back. He reaches in and holds the weighted item in his hand.

Matthew is hesitant but at the same time intrigued. This is the first time he has seen this book. Opening the cover, he begins flicking through the pages. He sees page after page of scrawled words. A moment or so passes before he realises the words have been written by his daughter. Breathing in deep, not feeling ready for the potential realities this may bring, Matthew slams the book of secrets closed and throws it onto the passenger seat. He sits with his head in his hands, unsure if he truly desires to read the full contents of the pages. After allowing his mind a brief moment to consider what could potentially be written there, he gives in. Before he knows it, Matthew has picked the book back up and is reading one of Evelyn Jade's entries.

I never thought in my entire life I would be this angry. Why doesn't he listen, or not even listen, but, like, just at least try and understand what I'm going through? Josie suggested it's time to tell dad, it's time to speak up and tell him how suicidal I am. Tell him exactly how much I no longer want to be alive. Tell him how I'd rather be dead with you, Mum. But guess what? Surprise, surprise, I can't — because he doesn't want to hear it. Why can't I just scream at him how I feel? Why do I end up feeling bad? Like I'd be setting him back somehow, because he's clearly much better now. If he cared about me the way he says he does, then I should be able to tell him anything.

You're dead because of me, your own flesh and blood, and there's no getting away from that. Every single day at school I get bullied. Everyone knows I killed my own mum, and yet he still sends me there. How does he think that's going to make me feel...?

That's just it, though, isn't it? He doesn't care about how it makes me feel, so why do I care so much about how he feels? I'll tell you why — it's the guilt. I took you away from him.

Mum, I'm so sorry I destroyed our family.

I'm so sorry I was your daughter...

The ink is smeared in places where Eve's tears must have landed on the page. Feeling his daughter's pain and riddled with guilt himself, Matthew is unable to read any more. He slams the journal shut and throws the book of secrets across the car. Angry, tearful and frustrated, he grabs the bottle of vodka and gulps from it once more. He'd give anything to be able to console his daughter, but not only this — he now knows the truth about his family's fate, he knows who is to blame for destroying his family unit, for the death of his wife and the abduction of his daughter's soul. And yet, here is his innocent baby girl, even long after the tragic event, truly believing she killed her own mum.

Closing his eyes, Matthew sees his soulless wife lying with her eyes open in a pool of her own blood. The thick deep red substance gushes from the huge crack in her skull. His beautiful wife has already taken her last breath.

Squeezing his eyes tighter to try and remove the image from his mind, Matthew experiences another flashback, this one even more heart-breaking than the last. He sees his daughter in her horrific demonic state. Her skin tone is grey and she has deep lacerations all over her body, from which oozes a thick disturbing black substance. Her jet-black hair hangs heavy and equally parted around her face, dripping with the same sinister-looking liquid as she levitates towards him. He hears a loud crack. His daughter is dislocating her bones. As she snaps her neck Matthew's eyes shoot open, releasing him from this awful image before he throws up.

Matthew is utterly devastated. He feels a huge sense of responsibility for his family's unfortunate fate. If only he'd never purchased the heart-shaped locket. Just altering this one teeny-tiny decision could have, in his mind, changed their destiny in such a profound way.

As the traumatising flashbacks continue to resurface unbidden, Matthew grows angry. He punches the roof of the car, hits the window and the steering wheel. But punishing himself with pain won't change the fact that he never actually stood a chance. During the time when he had Evelyn Jade in his life, he didn't manage to console her, or even recognise the thoughts circulating in her mind. If he had, perhaps he could have convinced her that she was never in any way responsible for the death of her mother. Unable to turn back time, Matthew once again lashes out in frustration, repeatedly smacking his own head and shouting, "You stupid, stupid, stupid man!"

He technically has more blood on his hands than his daughter does. Unfortunately for Matthew, he can't change his reality. He realised this way too late, and now that he's so far away from finding Evelyn Jade, he's lost it all. Pulling out his wallet he looks at the school picture of Evelyn Jade. "I'm so sorry, kidda," he says. "I never knew you were suffering so badly. I'm so sorry I let you down. I'm sorry you were stuck with me as your dad."

Wiping his face and holding back his remaining tears, Matthew clears his throat and regains his composure. Flicking down the sun visor and pushing back the small cover to reveal the mirror, Matthew's horrified by the man he sees in the reflection. He's unidentifiable. Looking himself straight in the eye he says, "What have you become?"

Unable to answer his own question but certain he doesn't like any part of the man he sees, his frustration turns into a surge of determination. Determination not to let his daughter down anymore. Looking himself dead in the eye, he says, "Matthew Honey, are you going to continue to sit back and do nothing? You're being treated like a victim because you're behaving like one. The only victim in your life is your daughter. Are you gonna be a man and go find her, or are you gonna carry on gettin' mugged off...?!" He pauses, as though he's waiting for an answer to his question. Once again staring himself deep in the eyes, he continues, "If you die, so what? At least you died trying to fight for your daughter and your freedom. It's. Time."

With his pep talk over, Matthew slams the sun visor back, shoves a mint in his mouth and bangs the car door shut. He sets off to see the people he detests the most: the authorities.

CHAPTER THREE

The Enemy

Matthew's thoughts whirl around his mind at a hundred miles per hour as he approaches the station. He has no clue how he's even going to begin to find his daughter; all he's clear on is that he will die trying. Entirely lost in the moment, before he knows it, he's reached his destination. Standing at the doorway, Matthew sighs heavily as he focuses on the task in hand. He hesitantly takes one step forward. Gathering all his will power, with his head down low Matthew doesn't make eye contact with anyone as he slowly walks through the front entrance of Lymington Police Station. The corridors have a sterile chemical smell, along with a mixture of male and female perfume. It's heaving with police force employees who impolitely and forcefully push past him as they rush around the building. The energy throughout seems urgent and fast paced. The walls are adorned with billboards advertising the local most-wanted list, and there are surveillance cameras in every corner. Shoved from one side of the corridor to the other, Matthew once again breathes in deeply, attempting to stay calm. He walks through the huge stiff double doors and makes his way to the reception desk. Matthew hears two cockney voices. Behind the navy-blue four-foot-tall counter there are two familiar faces. These two officers of the law, from Matthew's experience, are the complete opposite of one another.

"Collins, Collins, have you seen the logbook for the cells? Chief Inspector Lamont is going to ask for them and we need to make sure that they're up to date," says one of the officers, a short, gentle, middle-aged man. He looks at his colleague, who appears to be engrossed in his phone, then taps him on the arm. "Collins, seriously this is not a joke. Where's the cells logbook?" he says with a frustrated tone as he faffs around with some paperwork on the desk.

"Hahaha, 'ave a look at dis den, D'amo, check this picture some girl just sent me," PC Collins says, laughing and waving his phone at his colleague. "How hot is she, right?"

"You're so immature. What is it with your technology generation? Why do you insist on sending constant raunchy images of yourselves to one another?"

"Just fun, innit?" PC Collins replies, shrugging his shoulders.

Both officers remain seated, peering over the counter. The reception area is immaculate. The blue lino floor is freshly buffed, shining to perfection. A white and red line denotes a one- and two-metre gap around the counter. Matthew, aware of the procedure, is standing the appropriate distance away, his feet firmly inside the two white footprints marked on the floor. He has absolutely no desire to give these officers any reason to place him back into another one of their basic, twenty-four-hour surveillance, freezing cold cells.

Finally lifting his head from his phone, PC Collins says, "Aye, Honey, what a shame ya could make it. An' 'ere's me thinkin' I'm gonna 'ave the absolute pleasure of nickin' ya ta'day. Chief Inspecta Monty as even come in just in case. What. A. Shame. He will be gutted."

"Leave it out, Collins. Matthew, you're bang on time," PC D'amo says, smiling.

"Ya know the rules by now, Honey," PC Collins barks. "Get ya hoodie an' hat off!"

Closing his eyes and breathing deeply to try to conceal the pain he feels, Matthew lifts his arms to remove his hood and beanie hat. No sooner have they come off, PC Collins, without a professional or compassionate bone in his body, says tauntingly, "Oh, would ya look at dem beauties, ha! Dey've made a righ' mug outta ya, ain' dey den."

"Seriously, Collins, leave it out! Matthew, have you seen someone about your injuries?"

"No. I'm fine. Can we just get this over with, lads?"

"But…"

"No buts, I just want to leave."

Just at that moment, D'Amo jumps at the sight of his superior walking behind the counter.

"Oh, erm, Chief Inspector Lamont, sir, we're just sorting Matthew Honey's bail."

"I know who this one is, PC D'amo, there's no need for introductions," Chief Inspector Lamont replies in a strong, husky voice.

"Of course, sir."

The inspector looks smart in a navy-blue suit with a crisp white shirt and pink tie, but the expensive material is entrenched with a stale stench of cigarette smoke. His husky voice is probably due to his forty-a-day habit, Matthew surmises. With a smarmy smirk plastered across his face and his head held high, the square-shouldered, tall figure making his way towards Matthew is the designated Senior Investigating Officer, or, in Matthew's view, the enemy – Chief Inspector Lamont. He showcases a full head of blonde hair and the most piercing blue eyes. Even the stubble on his face has been perfectly trimmed, Matthew notes. And he clearly has only one desire at present: to put Matthew Honey behind bars for all eternity.

"So, Matthew Honey, would you look at the state of your mug shot." He begins sniggering under his breath. "Grantin' you bail again, are we? What a shame. I was gonna offer you a bed and some housekeeping." Looking to PC Collins he continues, "We could 'ave kept him away from the big bad bullies, couldn't we, Collins?"

PC Collins doesn't seem so cocky anymore as he says with a nervous tone, "Ha, yes, sir."

"Never mind, Honey, it looks like you're gettin' exactly what you deserve on the streets."

Clearly enjoying the power, Chief Inspector Lamont takes the clipboard from off the desk and says, "I tell ya what, step into this room here, Honey. I'll tick your bail sheet for you."

Lamont opens the door to one of the interview rooms, and Matthew sighs as he follows the enemy inside. Reaching to the switch on the wall next to the doorframe, Chief Inspector Lamont flicks on the light and closes the door behind him. Matthew is unimpressed by the position he has unexpectedly been forced into. The small dingy room has no windows or natural sunlight. The walls are the same depressing dark shade of blue as the reception area and have been plastered with crime advisory posters, along with the policing complaints procedure and "know your rights" information. Matthew can't help but feel this reading material is irrelevant, given the way he continues to be treated. Standing in the middle of this freezing cold, sterile room is an old unfashionable dark wooden table with four matching dark oak wooden chairs around it. The enemy moves closer, and Matthew knows what's coming next. He also knows he isn't going to like one single bit of it.

"Take a seat."

Rebelling against the instructions, Matthew replies, "Can we just get this over with? You and I both know I don't have to go through this with you in here. I can walk out of here right now if I like. You've seen my face. I'm certain there will be CCTV evidence to prove I've attended, so why don't you just stop right now and save us both the trouble?" There is a brief silence. Rolling his eyes, Matthew continues, "Come on, what do you want, Monty?"

"I said – I want you to take a seat, Honey."

Pulling the chair in frustration, Matthew sits at the table, attempting to control the rage that's building inside of him. Folding his arms to signal his lack of acceptance, Matthew scowls across the room at the enemy. Chief Inspector Lamont slams the clipboard on the table and puts his hands in his pockets; he remains standing. Staring down at Matthew he once again basks in his power.

"So, when are you gonna cut the shit, Honey, and just fess up? Or are you still tryin' to play the innocent card? Which you and I both know is total B.S."

Matthew choses to say nothing. There is absolutely no reason to respond. No good can come from speaking to this man, he's trouble.

"Oh, that's interesting, the silent card is it today then, Honey? You do know it's only those who have stuff to hide that say nothin', don't ya?" He pauses, waiting for Matthew to answer. With nothing but an awkward silence, he decides to continue, "Come on, Honey, we both know you killed your wife and then got rid of your kid, don't we now?"

At these words Matthew's posture changes slightly. It doesn't escape Lamont's notice.

"You know what I don't get, though?" he goads. "Why? I mean, alright, that wife of yours might have been a nag—"

At this Matthew jumps up, the chair producing a toe-curling screech as it scrapes back across the floor.

"Oh, hit a hot spot 'ave I…? Go on, what you gonna do 'bout it, big man?"

Breathing rapidly with frustration and once again gritting his teeth, Matthew closes his eyes and manages to regain control of his emotions as he sits back down. He has got too much to lose by giving this bully the smack in the face he deserves.

"That's it, you be a good boy and sit back in your naughty seat."

Lamont is laughing hysterically, clearly utterly amused with his taunting methods. Appearing satisfied with Matthew's reaction, he collects the paperwork from the table.

"Well, what do we have here, then? Bail terms and conditions for Matthew Honey. I don't know who you're payin' off to get this, but I promise you, I'm gonna do everythin' in my power to find out how and why you've done what you've done. And then, I'm gonna ensure you never walk the streets again. You just watch your back, Honey!"

Fed up with his bullying ways, Matthew bites back. "You just keep trying. You'll be the fool when I prove my innocence. And, when I do, because I am innocent, the first thing I'm going to be sure of is that you get stripped of your job and lose all your power, you pathetic bully. So I suggest you just watch your back, Monty! Now are you going to tick my name so that I can leave, please? Or are you charging me with something? If so, I want my lawyer present, you utter joke."

Biting his lip and retrieving the pen from the internal pocket of his jacket, Chief Inspector Lamont leans over the table and reads Matthew his brief bail terms and conditions. Once finished, he ticks Matthew's name and writes his initials next to this. Collecting the clipboard from the table, Chief Inspector Lamont leans right into Matthew's face as he says, "I will get you. You're one sick puppy, and I promise to get justice for your poor innocent wife and kid. I am always watching. Wherever you go, I won't be far away. Whatever you say, I will always be listening. You will fuck up. Everyone leaves a trail, no matter how good they think they are."

Feeling sick at the stench of second-hand cigarette smoke on this bully's breath, Matthew replies, "Get out of my face."

"Or what, big man?"

Getting to his feet, Matthew pushes his own face forward, "I don't have to tell you. You already think I'm a murdering scum bag, so all I have to say is – don't you push me."

"Wanna have some fun, Honey? Believe me, I don't need to push you. You are a scum bag and I'm gonna 'ave that horrid little mug shot of yours all over the globe by the time I've finished with you. Now get out my station."

"With pleasure."

Matthew heads for the door. Before leaving the room, he turns and looks at the enemy, who is standing tall and staring down his nose at him. He crosses his arms as he watches Matthew leaving the room. Pausing with his hand on the door handle, with his back turned, Matthew shares his final thoughts. "I'm going to find my daughter. Like you said, everyone leaves a trail. My advice to you: don't continue your attachment with your desk or colleagues. I will win this war you've started. That's a promise."

"Be seeing you soon."

Putting his hat back on his head and pulling his hood up, Matthew leaves the police station.

CHAPTER FOUR

See You on the Other Side

"What time are you both coming home?" Alice Parkinson says into the phone wedged precariously between her shoulder and ear as she makes her way into the dining room, juggling a handful of laundry. She waits for her stroppy teenage son to reply.

"I don't know, later."

"Right... okay... so will you be having supper?"

"I said I don't know."

Unimpressed with his response and tone, she continues, "I told you, Lewis, you both must be home before it gets dark."

"Mum, I'm sixteen now you can't just—"

"Listen," Alice interrupts. "I don't care that you've turned sixteen. What you need to understand, Lewis, is that there are four other children who live in this house. They're all a lot younger than you, and guess what?" She pauses, but not for long enough to give him a chance to answer. "I have to look after them, too."

"Yeah, I'm not stupid, Mum, I do know that. We'll be back by midnight."

"Categorically, no way! Lewis, I'm not staying up all night worrying about you both. Just make sure you're back before dark."

"Well, eleven, then?"

"Lewis, this is not up for discussion."

"Fine!"

"Thank you… See you later, son. I love you."

Alice throws the mound of laundry onto the solid dark oak dining table and drops the phone next to the heap. Surrounded by pile after pile of clean laundry, Alice shakes her head and rolls her eyes. This is often her expression following a conversation with her teenage son. She pushes her overgrown fringe out of her eyes, catching a whiff of baby sick mixed with sweet perfume on the sleeve of her long red and white chequered boyfriend shirt as she does so. How did she come to look so neglected at thirty-six, she wonders, looking down at her casual black leggings. Pulling her long dark brown hair, which is flecked with blonde, into a ponytail, she breathes in deeply, inhaling the strong scent of freshly washed clothing that is lingering in the air. She looks around at the dining room. It might be cluttered, but at least it's clean. Three of the walls are painted light grey, and opposite the double wooden glass-paned doors sits an elegant vintage-style centre piece in pastel colours. Alice commissioned a local talented designer to create the exclusive one-off creation.

This room was once the heart of the Parkinson home. The only time every member of the family came together was at mealtimes. At least twice every week religiously, they would all get together and sit around the family table to simply enjoy one another's company. Alice sighs as she remembers how she would constantly be trying to keep the little ones sat on their chairs and preventing food fights during, in her words, "feeding time at the zoo". Admittedly, most of the time this was because her husband, the family clown, had started a food fight, especially when peas were on the menu. There was warmth, laughter and love. This family unit was strong. Well, that's what they thought. Now, Alice reflects, the energy within this room is very different. Now, all this room holds are memories and a place to sort the clean clothes. No more food fights, no more games and no more planning for the future. This table will never again be complete. One of the grey painted walls showcases family photograph after family photograph, the Parkinson shrine dedicated to the missing family member, Phil Parkinson. The head of the family.

As she turns back to her mammoth task of folding clothes, Alice begins humming along to a familiar, jolly theatrical song coming from the television in the front room. The volume is almost at maximum, the children's programmes blaring out through the speakers. A hyperactive colourful entertainment show keeps the little ones highly amused with singing and dancing, replaying the same annoying illustrations on a loop every day. Alice realises that this hypnotising channel isn't the best for her little ones, but any such concerns are outweighed by the level of quiet she receives as it occupies their little minds.

At present, although times are mentally challenging for the Parkinson tribe, the innocence of the young makes it hard for the adults to be consumed by grief. These mini family members are fast paced and remain solely dependent on the adults surrounding them. Stopping her task and standing still for a brief moment to gather her thoughts, Alice peers out of the window. Gazing at the serenity of the sky, and taking in the peaceful ambience, suddenly, within the clouds, Alice sees a huge vibrant rainbow appear. This beautiful addition to the sky is so big it deceives her mind. It's so close, it appears as though she could jump straight through it. This breath-taking creation makes Alice feel warm inside as she quietly says, "Hey, baby." Alice's eyes begin to smile as she daydreams about happier times.

Snapping out of the vision, Alice brings her focus back to reality and the task in hand as she grabs her next item of laundry from the pile. Hearing the pitter-patter of footsteps on the wooden flooring, Alice peers over her shoulder to the doorway.

"Mummy, I hungry now."

Smiling, she places down the item of washing she was folding and makes her way across to the door. Kneeling down, she says, "Oh, really! Come here, my mummy's baba. Are you hungry here?"

Tickling her four-year-old ray of sunshine Terence on the tummy, Alice continues her loving attack by dramatically pretending to eat his stomach, then begins kissing his cheeky chubby baby face. Terence can't hold it in any longer and begins giggling loudly.

Continuing to chuckle he says, "Mummy, you can't eat me. *I* hungry, not Mummy hungry."

Once again feeling warmth in her heart at hearing her handsome boy speak, Alice sits on the floor and places him on her lap. Squeezing him tightly she begins singing the nursery rhyme song she created when Lewis was born. The same song which she has sung to every single one of her children, "You are amazing... you are amazing... I... love... you... I do..." Looking across to Rupert, who is also making his way into the dining room, she sees he's holding onto something he shouldn't be. "Oh, ah, ah, ah, Rupert. Put that down, my little prince, we don't play with that."

Placing Terence on the floor next to his little brother she takes the plug from the hoover out of two-year-old Rupert's hand just as it is about to make its way into his mouth. Dragging the heavy household appliance out of harm's way she says, "Right, what shall we put on the TV, boys?"

Terence instantly shouts, "Watch Sam Sam, the firing man."

"You wanna watch Sam Sam?"

In perfect symphony both Terence and Rupert shout out, "Yeah."

Walking with the boys into the front room, which is coated with layers of children's toys, Alice switches the television channel over to their favourite programme so that she can continue her household chores, hopefully this time, undisturbed. Smiling as the boys are now content, she walks back down the long hallway and resumes her position in the dining room. No sooner had she picked up her next item to fold she hears, "Mum...! Mum...!"

"I'm in the dining room, Freddie. And shhhh, you'll wake your sister, she's sleeping."

Alice's second-born son, Freddie, rushes into the dining room. Covered in dirt and looking like he just climbed down from a tree, the scruffy eight-year-old quietly says, "Sorry."

"It's fine, son. What's wrong?"

"Nothing. When's the food ready? And what time do I have to be home?"

"Your dinner will be ready around six and I want you home before then."

"Sweet, I'm going back to Jack's for a bit, then."

Not hanging around for his mum to change her mind, Freddie heads straight down the hallway to get back outside to his friend. He is almost out the house when Alice shouts, "Don't be late, Freddie, and don't slam the d—" The door slams before she has time to finish.

"Mummy. Me, Rupert and Sam Sam hungry."

Huffing to herself at this further interruption but laughing at his innocent scavenging attempts, she replies, "And Sam Sam?"

"Yes, and Rupert, and me."

"Okay, well, you, Rupert and Sam Sam can have some veggie sticks because dinner will be ready soon."

As she walks into the kitchen, Alice reaches into the huge American-style double-doored black fridge freezer. Following her into the kitchen, an innocent expression on his face, Terence jumps up and down with excitement as he waits for his mummy to appear with his veggie treats. She removes a child-sized blue plastic plate from the fridge. This has a variety of healthy and colourful snacks and is covered in cling film to keep the treats fresh. It's coated with layers of bright orange carrot sticks, juicy green cucumber slices and red peppers. On the side of the plate is a generous dollop of cream dipping sauce. Peeling the cling film off, she passes this to Terence, who says, "Dank you, Mummy," and begins to make his way back into the living room.

Carefully carrying his plate of colourful treats, Terrence puts this down on the small wooden square table in front of the TV. He pulls out his big boy chair and seats himself. Engrossed in Sam Sam the firing man, he begins munching away without a second thought to Rupert being hungry. Eating the carrot sticks like a little rabbit, Terrence begins chuckling away at the TV. As Rupert makes his way across to the table to get his fair share, Terrence chucks two of the cucumber sticks onto the floor. "Dat's Rupert's. D'ese mine."

"Ah, ah, now, now, Terence, you share. They're not just for you."

Alice is about to distribute the snacks out equally between the boys, but before she has chance to, her phone rings. Assuming this is Lewis mithering to stay out past midnight, she runs back into the dining room to answer the call. Surprised at the name flashing on the screen she says, "Oh, hi, Mum."

"What's wrong? You sound flustered."

"Nothing. Sorry, I thought it was Lewis... Everything okay?"

"Yes, my dear, I'm just checking on you and the children."

"Yeah, we're fine. Well, I'm just attempting to sort the house out."

"Do you need me to call round? Actually, I'll just call round."

"Mum, I don't need you to call round, it's fine. I'm fine. The children are fine."

"Are you sure? Honestly, my dear, you sound busy. I can just sit with the children for a bit and help out."

"Mum, honestly, I'm fine."

"Okay. If you're sure, my love. So, where is he?"

"Who?"

"You know I don't want to speak his name."

"At some point you're going to have to, because despite what you think, he's going nowhere."

"Well, not right now, I don't. He's preying on you because you're not strong at the moment. I know a controlling man when I see one – lord knows I put up with your father for all those years. Horrible man he was, too. And don't even get me started on that daughter of his. What a strange girl! Something just doesn't sit right with them two, and I'm telling you now, Alice, that girl is going to be a terrible influence over our young Lewis – mark my words."

"Right, let's not even go there, Mum. Seriously – his daughter? You're really going to pick a fight and start slagging off a child? Can we get off this conversation now? You and I both know where this gets us and I'm too tired to argue."

"Argue? Who's arguing? I'm your mother I have a right to be worried about you and the children. So where is he, then?"

"Oh, please just don't start, mother. *Jesse* is actually upstairs sorting Hope out."

"*Sorting Hope out! You've left him alone with Hope?* Oh, Alice, if Phil could see you now he'd be furious. You're leaving his one and only daughter to be put to bed by a strange man who she doesn't even know."

"*Well, Phil isn't here is he, Mum?* And, for your information, she does know Jesse thank you very much. She's my daughter and I'm more than capable of trusting my instincts on who I leave her alone with. Plus, she's taken to Jesse. She settles easier with him than she does me."

"Oh, I worry about you, Alice. I worry about all of you."

"Well, you don't need to. I'm a grown woman, Mum. I am a mother to five children, in case you hadn't noticed. I do know what I'm doing."

"Alice, you have a broken heart, my love. No one can truly function with a broken heart. You shouldn't be with this man – the timing isn't right. Actually, the whole situation isn't right. He's not right for you, I know it."

"Mum, we've been over this. Are you just trying to piss me off? I've told you to leave it."

"No, never, I'm just worried, Alice. You've all been through so much and I just want to be there for you all."

"I know you're worried, but really, Mum, you don't have to be. Listen, I've got to go and sort the boys out."

"Well, shall I call round later?"

"Only if you'll be nice."

"Okay, I promise, I will. I love you, darling, see you later."

"See you later. Love you, too."

Once again rolling her eyes and shaking her head, Alice puts the phone down and sits at the dining table. With her hands over her face, she breathes deeply, remembering the times when life wasn't so complicated. She smiles but it doesn't reach her eyes, and she sighs.

She is caught off guard by a clear vision appearing in her mind, a memory of her and her husband. They're lying in bed one early Sunday morning gazing at one another deep in thought whilst embracing each other's freckles, tiny laughter lines and individuality. Alice truly thought this was it, she was set for life. She'd found and married her soulmate. Everyone who knew the Parkinsons envied their huge loving family unit. Well, they don't anymore. Now they put their heads down with empathy at the sight of Alice Parkinson. The single widowed mother of five. A woman who has been forced into living this life by circumstances way out of her control.

Snapping out of her vision and regaining her composure, Alice heads to the front room. Peering in and seeing that the boys are perfectly content with snacks and Sam Sam the firing man, she walks to the staircase and closes the children's safety gate at the bottom after her. Tip-toeing, she heads towards Hope's bedroom. She slowly twists the doorknob in case her baby girl is sound asleep inside. As she enters the room, she smiles at the sight of Jesse, pausing for a moment to appreciate this very attractive, masculine male. With an impressive height of six foot four inches, he looks like a giant leaning over Hope's white wooden cot. His wavy, surfer-dude style, shoulder-length dark blonde hair is tied in a bun, with two front pieces draped on either side of his face. His facial bone structure is strong and his jawline is prominent, with stubble perfectly sculpted in all the right places to accentuate his features. Wearing a light blue polo t-shirt and dark denim Levi jeans, he pulls off the casual look with ease. He's almost a mirror image of Alice's deceased husband. Using all his concentration he's in a trance, gazing intently at six-week-old baby Hope as she sleeps. Under his breath, he's humming a familiar nursery rhyme. At the sound of a creak at the doorway, he breaks his contact with Hope and turns. Seeing Alice creeping into the room with a big grin on her face, he smiles from one side of his mouth and his deep brown eyes light up. Alice tip-toes her way across to Jesse so as not to disturb her daughter and places her head on to his shoulder as she too begins to gaze at her precious baby girl. Feeling content and proud she whispers, "Thank you."

Kissing her on the head, Jesse replies, "For what?"

"I suppose, for being you... for being so good with the children... for... well... for just everything, really."

Reaching his arms around her body he squeezes her tightly. "I'm here for your children."

With her head on his chest she's breathing him in. Closing her eyes tight and wrapped within his strength, Alice feels protected and safe. She feels as though the path she's on has had the curse lifted. She's no longer alone and vulnerable. She and her children have protection, they have Jesse. Opening her eyes, she looks back to her daughter. She is sleeping peacefully, resembling a sweet angel, surrounded by pure white sheets. Just above Hope's head sits a pastel pink fluffy teddy bear. This special man-made toy was left to this precious little girl by her daddy. This six-week-old baby never had the opportunity to meet the man who should have been her first true love, her daddy. He very sadly died before she was born. Before this baby girl had a chance to take her first breath, Phil Parkinson had already taken his own life. With her fate mapped within the stars, Hope was to remain fatherless for life. Phil had left this personalised teddy bear next to a suicide note, with wishes for his only daughter's name. The same name which was sewn onto the bear's stomach. And so, in honour of her husband, Alice named their only daughter Hope Eva Lia Parkinson. Whispering to Jesse once more, she says, "She's so pretty."

Hearing the quiet tone of her mum and still dreaming, Hope begins to fidget. Sucking her huge pink diamanté pacifier and making baby mumbling sounds, Hope moves her head slightly and Alice notices a deep black smudge on the cot sheet next to her head.

"What's that?"

Looking slightly sheepish, Jesse replies, "What?"

"That…" Leaning into the cot, Alice sees a black stain approximately the size of an English fifty pence piece. She touches it and the substance instantly sticks to her finger and tints her skin like black ink. Shuddering, Alice attempts unsuccessfully to wipe it off. Feeling physically sick, she says, "*Ew, ew, ew! That's disgusting.*"

"Sshh. You'll wake Hope."

Wanting to get the freezing cold nauseating liquid from off her skin, Alice rushes out of the bedroom to go and wash her hands.

CHAPTER FIVE

Power

Alone once more with Hope, Jesse tucks the sheets securely under Hope's chin. Once satisfied, he strokes her warm, slightly rosy, chubby cheek and follows Alice out of the bedroom. Turning back one final time, he stares at Hope before gently shutting the door behind him.

He enters the bathroom, where Alice is standing at the sink. The hot tap is flowing at maximum capacity, the steam from the water hitting the mirror just above the sink and is coating it with a mist. Preoccupied, Alice doesn't see Jesse enter. She's aggressively scrubbing her fingertip with soap; the dark, tainted looking liquid is refusing to leave her skin. Alice jumps as Jesse leans over her shoulder.

"My goodness! Jesse, you scared me then." Still struggling to remove the substance, she continues, "What is this? It won't come off."

Saying nothing, Jesse leans to Alice's neck and kisses it gently. As his breath lands on her skin, Jesse can see tiny pimples making an appearance.

As Jesse kisses her neck, Alice becomes stiff. Every part of her body has locked and become frozen. She can't act upon the words rapidly travelling around her mind. This internal, strong and loud voice is telling her to run and not look back.

Suddenly a thick substance manifests at the back of her throat. Alice tries but fails to swallow, and as it spreads and takes over her larynx, Alice begins to choke. She can't shift the substance, and it begins to fill her airways, bringing with it an overbearing, nauseating smell. It can only be described as the stench of death. She realises that she no longer has any power over her emotions or movements. Something is taking over her being.

Jesse is satisfied with Alice's quick submission. He very teasingly whispers into her ears, "Do – you – like – to play games – Ms Parkinson?"

Alice remains immobile and says nothing, her eyes closed. Jesse kisses her neck once more. The acceptance from her soul is almost complete. Suddenly, his eyes begin to turn a deep shade of grey. Embracing every second and the power he has, Jesse licks his way up her neck to her earlobe. Placing his hand on her chest, Jesse feels Alice's heartrate is no longer beating in sync. It has become erratic. This vital human organ is pounding rapidly. Her eyes are still closed, and Jesse feels the transition as he traps Alice deep within her own mind.

Aware he now has full reign, and placing his hands flat on her hips, Jesse grips this skeletal body part tightly. Aroused by his power, Jesse begins thrusting himself aggressively against her body, moaning under his breath. He leans close to her ear and whispers in a deep, dulcet, intimidating tone, "Oh, you want this don't you, Ms Parkinson?"

Aware that she doesn't have the ability to reply or even react to the violation of her body, Jesse is becoming aroused at the power he has. His erection is growing inside his jeans with every second that passes. Jesse has a huge desire to place himself forcefully and deep inside of her. Guiding his hands down to her crotch area, he holds this sensitive body part in his hands. Once again, Jesse whispers premeditated words directly into her ear and becomes present deep within her mind. "Now you have surrendered to me, I want to hear you moan."

Alice says no words but moans under her breath. Basking in the supremacy he has over the moment and getting a thrill as she adheres to his command, Jesse says, "That's it, you're a good girl."

Rubbing her clitoris from the outside of her thin leggings, Jesse feels the material is damp. Her body is accepting the tingling sensation and is becoming wet with pleasure. Continuing his dominant, intrusive and controlling ways, he says, "I command you to receive me."

As soon as his words are spoken, Alice throws her head on to his chest and moans louder than the last time. Alice is completely unaware of what is happening. She's unaware that she is in fact, surrendering a tiny molecule of her soul to this individual. Jesse's now content with his actions and Alice's acceptance. He smiles conceitedly and then makes his next calculated move. He says the four words you never wish to hear: "Your soul is mine…"

Alice moans louder. Continuing with the circling motion around her clitoris, Jesse is teasing her. Alice is trapped in the moment, under Jesse's command. He allows her the ability to speak, but her voice is deep and doesn't sound like her own as she says, "I want you inside me now."

Gyrating her body, she says, "I beg you, come deep inside me!"

Kissing her neck forcefully, Jesse is hard and thriving off the supremacy he feels at the full control he holds over the moment. Remaining behind Alice he thrusts upon her fully clothed body with intensity. Sensing she's about to climax and wanting to keep full reign over the moment, he releases her genitalia from his hand. Gripping her hair in his hand, he pulls her head back and nibbles at the skin on her neck as he says, "All in good time… for now, you have served your purpose. You have passed the test."

Loving the control he has and wanting to physically see her hurting Jesse commands, "Cry, I want to see your pain."

No sooner have the words left his mouth than a single tear rolls down the side of Alice's cheek.

"Remember one very important thing, Ms Parkinson: from this day, if I say so… you do so… Do you understand?"

"Yes."

Without an ounce of compassion, he pulls harder and grits his teeth as he says into her ear, "The deep flames of hell burning inside me love it when I hurt you, it turns me on."

Releasing her hair, he grips her crotch area harshly and thrusts up against her. Wanting full pleasure himself, Jesse begins undoing his jeans assertively and, just as he's about rip her leggings down to place himself deep inside of her, Jesse is caught off guard as the front door bangs shut!

The sound of the door slamming breaks Alice's entrapment, and she begins choking. She curls over the sink in pain, her head throbbing. Her body trembling, Alice is regaining consciousness and begins looking at her current state. Utterly mortified and confused, she says, "What's going on? Oh, my goodness, what on earth are we doing?"

"What do you mean? You were asking me to have sex with you."

"What?!" Pushing herself away from Jesse and back towards the bathroom door she says, "Why was... I... erm... I don't understand?" She places her head in her hands, and as she touches her scalp it feels tender and sore. Scrunching her face at the pain, she says, "I'm sorry... erm... I honestly don't know what came over me."

Flinching slightly as Jesse reaches out to hold her, Alice is extremely alarmed.

"It's okay if you've changed your mind and you don't want to do this," Jesse replies. "I just wanted to give you what you asked for, my queen, and to make you happy. I only ever want to please you. I don't just want you for sex. I want your soul. I want your children. I want the whole package. You don't need to apologise. I'm going nowhere, don't you worry."

He kisses her on the forehead. They hear rustling bags coming from downstairs and compose themselves, rearranging their hair and clothing. Alice and Jesse begin to make their way out of the bathroom and down the stairs.

A familiar voice shouts out, "Hello! Alice?"

Terence and Rupert run out of the front room, shouting, "Nannie..." in perfect symphony.

Standing in the hallway is Alice's mum, Dorothy Davies. Wearing her trendy, casual, high street fashion clothing, Dorothy is younger than most grandmothers. She, like her daughter, was once a young teenage mum. In this respect, the family history seemed to repeat itself.

Dorothy, at the young age of fifty-two, a mother to just one, is now a grandmother, or nannie as she calls herself, to five. She embraces being a nannie. The same can't be said for her mothering abilities to Alice during her younger years. But she has a different outlook when it comes to her grandchildren. Dorothy is a committed trendy nannie.

She has thick, long, shiny, straight red hair and piercing green eyes, offset by her pale skin and slight freckles. This middle-aged woman is curvy and fabulous. In her hands she holds bags of treats and gifts for the children. As soon as Dorothy sees two of her precious grandsons she beams and shouts, "Hello my boys, there you are. Come and give your nannie a big hug." Squeezing the boys with all her might, she continues, "Where's mummy?"

Standing at the bottom of the stairs, flustered, Alice sees the concern in her mum's eyes.

"Alice..." Dorothy begins, trailing off when she sees Jesse appear not too far behind her. "Erm, oh, there you are. I've come to see if I can help you with anything."

Making her way over to her mum, Alice hugs her and greets her with a kiss as she says, "Mum, I told you we're fine."

Without acknowledging Jesse, Dorothy says to her daughter, "Don't be silly, I'm here now. Is Hope asleep? And where are Lewis and Freddie?"

"Yes, I've just got her off to sleep," Jesse cuts in. "And the boys are out. Can I get you anything to drink, Dorothy?"

"No."

Not wanting a scene, Alice sternly says, "Mum."

"Fine – no thank you." Quick to disengage with Jesse, Dorothy looks straight to Terence and Freddie. As she kneels down, she says, "Come on then, my precious little gents, what shall we do? Look, nannie has brought you toys."

Terence pulls her arm, obviously bursting at the seams with excitement, and shouts, "Yay! Nannie, look, Sam Sam firing man."

As they enter the front room, Jesse grabs Alice's arm and says, "Sort it or I will."

With his fingertips pressing deep into the soft muscle on her arm, Alice says, "Ouch, Jesse, let go. I'll sort it." Rubbing her arm to try and soothe the pain, Alice follows her mum into the front room wearing a fake smile worthy of an Oscar.

CHAPTER SIX

Who Are You Calling Chicken?

The alleyway is shrouded in darkness, the only light coming from the dim streetlamps, which are coated with graffiti. The crooked tainted-looking trail leads onto a huge overgrown field. Discarded waste lies on the ground like a blanket. Unwanted furniture has been randomly left around and multiple mounds of black ash from previous bonfires are spread out across the area resembling mole hills. In the distance, hidden within the shadows, stands an abandoned children's playground.

The playground is enclosed by a huge metal fence. The Council built it in the hope of keeping the public out. There are signs that say WARNING and DO NOT ENTER everywhere. But since there are no electric fences or real consequences to entering, the area has become a regular hang-out spot for troubled souls and disobedient youth. It's also a place where deprived addicts can shoot up undisturbed and the local homeless can sleep. It radiates an eerie energy. The once loved children's venue has most definitely become a place where you would never desire to take your precious young.

There is a metal slide that has dangerous shards of glass resting at the bottom, along with a defective see saw. No park would be complete without a swing set, except, this particular swing set is barely standing and it creaks eerily at the slightest breeze.

Lewis Parkinson is hanging out in the playground with his friends. They're surrounded by a sea of dirty needles, foil, and other drug paraphernalia left behind by the local addicts. The group of troubled teens are being disrespectful and destructive. From grabbing bottles and smashing them off the ground, to spray painting the surrounding brick walls, park fixtures and anything else that can they get their hands on, they have been behaving in a despicable manner. At present, they are sitting on one of the benches, listening to music and drinking copious amounts of alcohol.

"Neck it – neck it – neck it. Don't be a pussy, Ben."

"Shut your face, Lew. You know I've got Irish blood. As my dad would always say, 'Us O'Doyle's can drink any man under the table' I've done it before and will do it again. Don't tempt me cause you know I'll just embarrass your arse."

Left to their own devices, this teenage group isn't concerned about the darkness. They don't appreciate the fact that they're potentially in a very dangerous situation by loitering around an abandoned playground at night. They are unbothered by missed curfews and betrayals of parental trust.

"Go on then, throw it back."

"Fine – one, two, three…"

Ben puts the bottle of whisky to his lips and drinks the contents at a rapid rate. He gags as the alcohol travels down his throat and warms his stomach.

"Fuck me, that's just disgusting. We should have got vodka."

"Lew – look – you forgot your crack pipe."

Picking up one of the needles from the floor, Ben begins chasing Lewis around the park with it.

Frantic, Lewis shouts, "Mate, are you mad? You'll catch-AIDS, you fucking dick head. Put it down, man."

Ben throws the needle to the ground.

"Eww, mate, what if I've got the AIDS I don't want the AIDS. I'm too young to die."

"Mate, you're not going to die. Now come on, sort yourself out, you spaz."

They re-join the group, who are playing music through their phones and joking around together.

The reputation of this park doesn't bother Lewis one bit. This intimidating group of teenage lads and a single teenage girl are having fun by vandalising the area further and destroying whatever might have survived previous rampages. Lewis is the leader of the group and his friends are always battling for his approval and acknowledgement. They are an assorted group of misfits, each one troubled in some way.

Standing proudly with his head held high is Ben O'Doyle. Lewis never goes anywhere without Ben.

Ben has wavy dark brown hair, which he has caked with copious amounts of gel and various other products. It's flicked to one side, accentuating the trendy teenager's sharp cheek bones and youthful skin. With his bright blue eyes and Irish accent, Ben is popular with the young ladies.

Lewis and Ben have been tightly bonded since the very early years of pre-school. Together, these two have stood side by side through thick and thin. They are inseparable.

Then there's the sensible brains of the group, sixteen-year-old Hugo Newman.

"Lads, do you want some of this?" Hugo says as he waves a bottle of brandy in the air. "Lewis, Lewis, here, have some of this."

Lewis laughs as Hugo shoves the bottle in his face. "Mate, I'm good, I've got a beer."

"Suit yourself, then." Turning, Hugo makes a beeline for Ben. "Benny boy, do you want some of this brandy? It is top notch. I stole it from my father's collection in the basement."

"Yeah, go on then, mate. Nice one." Knocking back the straight brandy, Ben coughs.

"You pair of muppets," Lewis says, laughing.

"Ha, Benny boy, it would appear that you can't handle your drink. You're no match for the mighty Hugo," Hugo boasts, flexing his muscles.

When he joined Waverley Hey Academy three years ago, Hugo instantly connected with Lewis and Ben. With his quirky attitude, he added a different dimension to the dynamic. Desperate to fit in,

Hugo was quick to surrender his morals in order to have something he'd never been privy to before: friends. With his elegant English accent, extensive vocabulary and knowledge, Hugo doesn't exactly fit in with most school cliques, so when he secured his place with Lewis and Ben it was more than he ever dared hope for.

Once Hugo was in, Lewis was quick to realise that welcoming this member into his and Ben's dynamic enhanced their abilities and strengths dramatically. And so, when the house next to the derelict park that had been boarded-up for months became occupied by an oversized family, the boards were taken down and Lewis, Ben and Hugo were quick to recruit two of the new residents there, the genuine terrible twosome – fifteen-year-old identical twin brothers, Elijah and Isaiah Obi. With their tanned completion and dazzling smiles, Lewis believed Elijah and Isaiah were a perfect combination to add to his growing group of friends.

Elijah, who is sat at the other end of the bench, watches Ben coughing. "What is it?" he asks.

"It's super fucking strong brandy, mate," Ben says, his voice hoarse.

Ben passes the bottle to Elijah. No sooner has he gripped the neck of the bottle than he throws the intoxicating liquid to the back of this throat.

Digging inside his pocket on his jacket, Hugo pulls out a plastic bag.

"What's that you've got?" Lewis says, intrigued.

"Ah ha, you want to know what this is? Well, it's a little something special I have concocted for us to get a sweet little buzz."

"Mate, it looks like your nan baked it," Isaiah says, appearing amused.

"Oh boys, believe me, my grandmother doesn't bake this kind of product. Come on, have I let you down before? Huh…"

"Fuck it – I'm in," Elijah says.

Following in his brother's footsteps, Isaiah says, "Give me one of them."

"Isaiah, man, stop hogging the product, we wanna trip too," Elijah says as he snatches the bag from out of his brother's hands.

Curious, Lewis questions, "Hugo, what sort of buzz we gonna get from this?"

"Well, Lewis – let's just say in a moment or two you're going to feel the most immense rush throughout your body. These fluffy mini bites are what I like to call my pillows of euphoria."

"Yeah, man – Lewis, give me one of those pillows," Ben says.

"One-minute, Ben, chill, you're gonna knock em out me hand," Elijah complains.

"Boys," Hugo says in a calm voice, "relax, there's plenty to go around." He smirks as he takes another bag of the fluffy looking cakes out of his pocket.

"Elijah, can you feel that?" says Isaiah.

"What?" asks Elijah.

"That, my hand is moving."

"Isaiah, you need to sort your head out," Elijah says, laughing. "I can't feel shit. Hugo man what the fuck?"

"Be patient, it will come."

Lewis spots his friend across the park putting his phone back in his pocket after finishing a call. "Hey Renz, check out these pillows that Hugo's nan made," he shouts.

Making his way over is the smallest member of the group, sixteen-year-old Renato Da-Silva-Fernandes. He comes from a family of shorter males, but while his genes may have stunted his growth, his lack of height is not something others should mistake for a weakness. An only child, Renato is a spoilt hot head. With brown hair, deep chocolate brown eyes and olive skin complexion, Renato is originally from Portugal and came to the United Kingdom only seven years ago.

"What is it?" asks Renato.

"It's a pillow cake thing that gets you high. Look, my hand is floating," Isaiah says, waving his arm in the air. He looks like he's in a trance.

"Keep those things away from me, man. I've got a kick boxing competition this week I need to keep my title. If I have to get drug tested and whatever that shit is comes up, my dad will fucking kill me."

Every young male within the group has his own purpose and they each bring something unique to the table. Filled with testosterone, this group of friends are all currently competing for the undivided attention of the only girl present.

She has thick shoulder-length choppy jet-black hair that has been parted on one side and swoops across one of her eyes. Her hairstyle compliments her dark alternative clothing. This expressive young lady is embracing the rock chick look. At present, she's ordering the young impressionable boys to complete nuisance dares while she records them on her phone. Looking at Renato, she chuckles. In her extremely well-spoken English accent she says, "So, you won't take drugs because – daddy might kill you? Ha, let's see just how chicken are you then, mini man…"

Appearing to be instantly offended by her words and not used to being mocked by a girl, Renato responds, "Nar, chicken. Did you just say chicken? I'm no chicken, am I lads?"

The boys snigger under their breath at Renato being called out. An awkward silence ensues. Seemingly frustrated by this lack of backing from his friends, Renato becomes aggressive. "Nar! So it's like that then? You can all just shut up anyway. I'll show you lot chicken."

The young girl continues to record the events on her phone. Renato begins stomping around the park. Both Lewis and the trouble-causing young girl follow him out of the playground.

"So what you going to do then, mini man?" the girl taunts.

"Mini man? Pfftt, you wanna stop calling me that or I'll show you mini man."

"Oh, you do know how to excite a girl, don't you, Renz?" she teases.

Lewis chases after Renato as he makes his way across the field.

"Renz, what are you doing?" Lewis pleads with his friend, concerned about what Renato might do next. "Come on, mate, don't be daft. Let's just go back to the park."

"Nar, mate, you'll see." Turning away, Renato mutters under his breath, "Fucking chicken. Stupid bitch, I'll show you fucking chicken."

Lewis watches as Renato grabs a huge black plastic sack from a pile of discarded waste. It is bursting at the seams. Following Renato back into the park, Lewis shouts, "Mate, come on, what are you doing?"

Renato grabs one of the seats on the baby swing set. It's barely hanging from rusty metal chains. The corroded frame looks as if it's going to come crashing down at any moment. Renato stuffs the rubbish bag into the seat.

"Come on then, what are you going to do with that? Tell the camera. Give us a wave," the girl says.

Renato doesn't respond. Taking a lighter from his pocket, he flicks the flint down and sets the plastic black bag alight. It instantly bursts into a huge ball of bright orange flames which begin travelling at a rapid rate. As Renato turns his back to the fire, he laughs loudly and shouts, "Yeah, who's chicken now?!"

Lewis and all the other lads stand, gobsmacked, watching the destructive fire gust up the frame of the swing set. Feeling the heat from the blaze, Lewis shouts, "*Renato, you muppet! What did you do that for?*"

"What?" Renato replies, seeming confused that his friends aren't cheering him on.

"Are you mad?" Lewis says. "We're all on our last strike. One more strike and we're all getting nicked. No more kick boxing career for you, ya fucking idiot."

Panicking, Lewis turns to the group. "We should get the fuck out of 'ere. Throw your hoods up. Don't forget, there's CCTV."

"He's a fucking dick head, man. What the fuck did he do that for?" Elijah says.

"No idea mate. You need to get Isaiah he's out of it," Lewis replies.

Grabbing his brother, Elijah begins shouting in Isaiah's face. "Yo, you need to fucking sober up cause we need to get the fuck outta here."

"Huh."

"Isaiah, snap the fuck out of it, Renz has started a fucking fire. The fucking pigs are gonna be on their way."

The girl doesn't engage with the group discussion. She is standing just a few feet away from the fire. Still recording the events, she stares intently, appearing to embrace this vicious fiery energy as it grows. She watches as all the elements inside the bag crumble in the flames. Stray sparks scatter and a lavalike residue trickles from the swing set, landing on the tarmac floor and beginning to burn the waste left on the ground. It's spreading fast. As all the different materials inside the bag continue fuelling the fire, a glow glistening in the reflection of the girl's eye. Smiling and appearing content at the events which are taking place, she doesn't so much as flinch as a sudden huge *bang* bursts from inside.

Hugo shouts, *"Aerosol can! Run!"*

The boys hear the sound of sirens in the distance. Panicking, Lewis runs to the girl in a desperate attempt to grab her arm and drag her away. In a trance like state, she doesn't move so much as an inch. Pulling on her arm again, Lewis shouts, "Come on, we need to get out of here. We're gonna get nicked for arson." Still no response. Lewis shakes her and shouts *"Move!"*

She appears to be utterly obsessed with the destructive growing energy. She closes her eyes and then gasps for air. Lewis continues calling her name. The sirens are getting louder with every second.

Shaking her one final time, Lewis shouts, "Come on, we need to run."

She turns to Lewis and begins laughing hysterically. Lewis sees the rest of the group have already disappeared. Holding her hand, Lewis grabs her phone, switches off the camera and begins running, pulling her alongside him. He looks across to her and sees she seems content, smiling from ear to ear. Lewis cannot help but wonder what is going on inside her head as the expression on her face doesn't match the situation. She's laughing and seems proud of the destruction they've caused. The further away they get from the crime scene, the less anxious Lewis feels. They are now far enough away to know that they have escaped without detection or any connection to the criminal activity behind them. Shaking his head in disbelief, Lewis breathes deeply. They almost got caught.

Staring back at the girl, Lewis is captivated by her beautiful features, which are revealed with each bounce of her hair as she runs alongside him. Lewis smiles as his final bit of anxiety turns into adrenaline.

Once the park is completely out of sight, they slow down. Lewis looks across to her once more. Slightly out of breath, she laughs loudly. Her laughter is contagious and Lewis joins in. They stop in the alleyway. Alone with this girl and aroused, Lewis is desperate to kiss her. Suddenly she pushes Lewis up against the wall and kisses him passionately. Unable to think, Lewis surrenders to her and his legs go weak. The sirens are getting louder, but these two don't so much as flinch as they become physically intertwined with one another.

CHAPTER SEVEN

Murderer!

Arriving back at home, Matthew is about to activate the automatic door to his garage but before he presses the button, he notices something isn't quite right. Stopping the car halfway down the drive, he looks at the front of the house. Confused, Matthew sees that the front door is not the way he left it. Apparently the "intruder-proof" sturdy door is no longer locked. It has been forcefully opened and vandalised. Staying in the car, Matthew stares attentively to ensure that his mind isn't in fact playing cruel tricks on him. Once his sight has confirmed that the door is wide open, he drives forward and pulls the handbrake up, while trying to remain calm. He is attempting to think rationally but struggling somewhat. Eventually he decides it's best to leave the car parked outside the garage as this entrance also leads directly into the house. His thoughts racing at a hundred miles per hour, Matthew is getting himself into a state of panic. His palms are becoming moist and his hands suddenly begin to tremble. His levels of anxiety are rapidly heightening as adrenaline surges through his body.

Tired of the games with which life continues to present to him, Matthew reaches into the glove compartment and grabs the bottle of vodka. Unable to calm his nerves by himself, Matthew is desperate for the toxic substance to take over and numb his mind. Undoing the metal cap, he throws the remaining contents of the bottle to the back of his throat. Closing his eyes and breathing in deeply, he feels the intoxicating liquid warming his internal organs as it travels through his body. Embracing the Dutch courage the alcoholic beverage gives him as it spreads around his system, Matthew now feels as if he can conquer his fear of going inside the house. Putting the strong urge to run away to the back of his mind, Matthew makes his final decision: he's entering the house. Throwing the empty bottle onto the passenger's seat, he wipes his mouth and attempts to motivate himself, "Right! Come on, Matthew."

Gathering his thoughts, he looks across the car and sees the brown leather backed diary resting in the footwell. Leaning over he struggles slightly as the pain from his broken ribs travels like a bolt of lightning up his torso. Wrapped up in the moment, he had forgotten all about his broken body. Picking up the diary, he holds it in his hands. Bringing the book of secrets up to his nose, Matthew smells the material to see if it has any trace of his daughter's scent. Just knowing that she once held this very same possession makes him feel that tiny bit closer to her. Closing his eyes, he kisses the leather cover and slips the diary into the inside pocket of his jacket. He is content with its positioning – this precious irreplaceable item of memorabilia is now resting against his heart. Desiring nothing other than to focus all his attention on the only challenge he truly wishes to face, which is finding his daughter, Matthew looks into the rear-view mirror, staring deep into his own eyes.

"You're running out of time! You know you have a bigger mission than this. If you can't face such a tiny challenge, what can you face? Now get a grip!"

His final mini pep talk over, Matthew reaches back into the glove compartment and this time grabs his pistol. He examines the gun to make sure it's loaded. Matthew steps out of the car and is cautious not to slam the door shut. He doesn't want to warn the potential intruders of his arrival. Making his way towards the house, he takes the deepest breath in. He's armed but very nervous. Unfortunately, whether he's confident or not, there's no going back now.

Reaching the house, Matthew's stands absolutely still, his back leaning against the front door. He can feel and hear every pump of his heart as it beats rapidly. Listening intently, Matthew's on high alert for any noise that any intruders inside might make. There is deafening silence inside the building. Along with his heartbeat, the only other thing Matthew can hear is the sound of his breath as it leaves his body. Slowly, he enters the hallway. It's so quiet you could hear a pin drop. Holding his arms high and the pistol in the defence position, Matthew feels a rush as adrenaline travels throughout his entire body with every step he takes.

He makes his way towards the day room. Each step he takes he places down with caution. He is desperate not to create any sound by stepping on the debris that's on the floor. Arriving at the day room, Matthew places his back up against the wall, and once again closes his eyes as he breathes deeply. His hands are trembling. Ready to face the unknown, Matthew jumps through the doorway. Scanning the room, much to his relief, he sees there is no one there. Entering this chaotic space, Matthew's sight is instantly drawn to the huge graffiti message that has been left for him. Fresh, bright red paint drips down the walls, displaying one single malicious word. This very same eight-letter word that continues to haunt him daily has been sprayed in capital letters: "MURDERER". Filled with a deep sadness and overwhelmed with misery, Matthew endures a huge sigh of despair as he slumps against the wall. Feeling weary of people's lack of compassion, he sits with his legs high and rests his arms on his knees. Dropping his pistol between his legs and onto the floor, Matthew puts his head in his hands and attempts to gather his thoughts. Trying not to sink back into a state of depression and yet again allow the ignorance of strangers to control his emotions, Matthew begins sobbing to himself. Tired of the torment, he's tempted to end it all.

After his findings, Matthew believed he was the only person inside the house, but suddenly he hears the sound of scurrying footsteps coming from upstairs. Without so much as a second thought, Matthew grabs his pistol and jumps up. Ready to face these pathetic vandalizing bullies, he heads out of the room and towards the bottom of the spiral staircase. He shouts out, "Who's up there? I've got a gun, I will shoot, I promise!" Without an answer, the footsteps can still be heard, "I'll give you one chance to get out of my house!"

No sooner have the words left his mouth than the banging stops. Anxiously waiting for a reply, and once again not receiving one, he shouts, "I know you're up there." Still no answer. "Fine – have it your way. I'm counting to five and then I'm coming up. One... two... three..."

He doesn't finish counting before the thudding starts again, except this time, it's getting louder and sounds like a stampede. Scared, Matthew quickly heads back into the day room. The intruders are now closer than ever. Shielding himself behind the wall, Matthew waits anxiously for whoever is upstairs to come down. Gathering his strength and perfecting his aim, he's ready to teach them a lesson. His hands trembling, Matthew is aware there's no going back.

Rushing and almost tripping over one another in a desperate attempt to get to the bottom of the spiral staircase unharmed, three individuals all wearing black hoodies and white face masks appear, heading directly towards Matthew. Freaked out by the appearance of the unknown individuals, Matthew pulls the trigger and aimlessly fires his pistol. But, lucky for the intruders, he completely misses. He hears one of them shout, "Shit! The nutter's got a gun. Quick, leg it, lads."

With the ringing still in his ears from the shot that has just gone off, Matthew struggles to keep his balance as he heads towards the front door to chase after the intruders. But he doesn't make it in time. The trespassers were way too quick and have gone out of sight completely. "Let that be a lesson to you. Stay out of my house," he bellows in the hope they can hear him.

Rage begins growing inside of him. Using all his strength, Matthew reaches for the door which is barely hanging on by its hinges and attempts to close it. Huffing and puffing, he lifts and shoves the heavy door with all his might. Hearing the click from the lock somehow connect, Matthew rests his head on the door with relief. As he tries to regulate his breathing, his legs become weak. The adrenaline levels in his body are rapidly plummeting. He sways slightly, his breathing erratic and heavy. Matthew stumbles across to the bottom of the spiral staircase. He's having a panic attack. With his eyes closed, he breathes deeply. He can feel every inhale and exhale in his lungs.

Opening his eyes, Matthew shouts, "Shit!"

His pistol still in his hands, he jumps up onto his feet and runs up the staircase as fast as he possibly can. Matthew is frantic. Graffiti has been sprayed on the walls throughout the house. It's so fresh, the paint is still dripping. He pays no attention to the words on the wall. With a fearful expression, Matthew kicks the debris and mess out of his way as he runs towards Eve's bedroom.

He's relieved to find the door is closed. Tired, Matthew places his head and his hands against the bedroom door and takes a moment to calm himself. Preparing for the worst-case scenario, Matthew turns the handle on Eve's bedroom door and enters the room.

Releasing a sigh of gratitude, he stands still. Tears begin uncontrollably welling in his eyes. Thankfully, the room remains untouched and is in the exact same state as it was when his daughter was last there. Not a single item leans so much as a centimetre out of place. Her bed is neatly made. Her clothes still hang in the wardrobe, organised by colour and season like a true work of art. Her violin is in its case, leaning at the end of the bed. Also untouched and proudly placed on the wall above the head of the bed is a heart mosaic. Slumped against one of the pillows on the bed with the same tired and lonely expression as Matthew is Gregg, Eve's bow-tied teddy bear.

Drained and crying, Matthew begins wiping his tears. He places his pistol on the bedside table and picks up the golden frame containing the image of his wife and his daughter on their last ever mum and daughter day together before his wife was deliberately and cruelly taken away. Holding this precious item in his hands, he sits on the edge of the bed.

"I'm sorry." Crying heavily, he continues, "I love you so much and I will keep my promise to you. I will search the ends of the world to find our baby girl. I will bring her home if it kills me." Kissing the image of his wife and daughter, Matthew places it back on to the bedside table and then lies back on the bed. Glancing across to Gregg, he holds the scruffy looking bear in his hands and speaks once more. "So, come on then, Gregg, where do we begin?"

A smile forms on Matthew's face as the ridiculousness of speaking to a stuffed toy dawns on him.

"Huh, is this what my life's come to? Confiding in a stuffed bear?"

Shaking his head, he looks across the room. He has been back inside Eve's room multiple times since she was taken, but he has clearly paid no attention to detail. Resting on her desk is a thick red leather-backed diary with a solid golden buckle. An item he's never noticed before. Placing Gregg back on to the bed, he makes his way to the desk and picks up the diary.

Much like earlier, he's hesitant about reading the contents of the pages. Sitting back on the bed he undoes the buckle and flicks through the sheets of paper. Seeing the same scrawled blue inked writing on each page, he instantly becomes emotional. He's nervous about reading this book of secrets. Turning to the last heart-pouring account, Matthew decides he's going to be brave and read his daughter's final entry inside this book, dated the sixth of July. Matthew reads the following:

"I feel different and I can't explain it other than I constantly feel angry and isolated. I've not experienced this level of distance between me and my dad for such a long time. Like, we could literally be strangers who share genetics and nothing more. I love him, well, I think I still love him. Why is this so hard? Help me, please, what's wrong with me? I'm so confused. Mum, please give me some guidance.

Honestly, the thought of my dad still breathing angers me. Every morning when I wake up I feel as though venom has been pumped inside my body while I've been sleeping and my level of hate and aggression towards my dad grows stronger.

It's my last ever school concert tomorrow. I'm so excited. This should be a positive father-daughter moment and yet I just know he's not going to be sat in his seat. I've already made my prediction – he's going to be so busy and wrapped up in his work that he's not going to give me so much as a second thought. He won't care that his daughter will be the only student playing to an empty chair.

And yet there's Jess! She can't do enough for me. I know she's going to come tomorrow to show her support; she's already told me she'll be there no matter what it takes. How can a stranger care more about me than my own dad? My own flesh and blood. If he doesn't come tomorrow, that's it, I swear I will completely give up on that man. I'll be letting go and living my life just like he is. I'll go places I've never been before and leave him with his film company. The man cares more about his staff than he does about his only daughter..."

The words on the page become blurry as the tears welling in his eyes begin uncontrollably gushing down his face. And, as each one lands on the page, the ink smears. Attempting to regain control of his emotions, Matthew's not ready to read the truth. He feels empathy for his daughter and angry that he didn't prioritise and support her achievements. Her words are a confirmation of his failings as a father. Matthew whispers, "No wonder she hates you. No wonder she was taken so easily. No wonder she was so unhappy." Feeling both anger and sadness, he wipes his face once more and looks again at the picture on the bedside table. His eyes on his wife's image, he continues, "I am so sorry. I should have died. You should have stayed with our daughter." He sobs louder than ever at this truthful recognition. "This would have never happened if you were here instead of me."

Utterly devastated by the words he's read and finally acknowledging his failures, Matthew sees exactly how he neglected his daughter when she truly needed him the most. Closing his eyes, Matthew sees Eve. She's standing with pride, shoulders back and centre stage. She's smiling and slowly looking through the audience to find him, but he's not in his seat. He can see and feel the anxiety building as she's both excited and nervous. Then, the reality hits. She looks, hoping to see him rushing through the audience to take his seat. His seat remains empty.

As he opens his eyes, a knot develops inside his stomach. He put his daughter through the pain and disappointment for what? A business, a job, ungrateful demanding clients who were never loyal to him, really? He's a let-down and now he knows it more than ever. Clearing the tears from his eyes once more, he's determined not to let

Evelyn Jade down any longer. No more excuses, no more weakness, it's time to prove to his daughter that she is everything to him. He's going to track her down, free her soul and bring her home! With the anger bubbling up inside of him, this powerful emotion mixes with the sadness he feels, and these two strong emotions combine and turn into determination.

"…at least I've got Jess from him. She's already told me she's here for me. And, you know like how I said I'm going to leave and go travelling? Well, Jess said she's got family who live up north here in the UK somewhere, I think it's about four hours or so away. She's promised to take me to visit and I believe her because she's not full of crap like my dad. I'm really excited. I've never been up north before…"

Matthew suddenly realises this may be the clue he needs to start his hunt. Slamming the diary shut and keeping it in his hand, he grabs his pistol along with Gregg and heads out of the room. Shutting the door behind him, he blows his ritual kiss.

CHAPTER EIGHT

Guess Who?

Scattered throughout the midnight sky, the stars are beginning to twinkle one by one. Night has officially fallen. The roads are clear and quiet. There is a subtle breeze just strong enough to ruffle the leaves on the trees. Streetlamps light the pavement. Hungry foxes are making an appearance, bravely running from garden to garden scavenging for scraps to eat. Not a single person is present. Owls hoot from the protection of the trees. Other than nature's nocturnal animals occasionally making their presence known, everything is calm and peaceful. But the same can't be said for the current ambience inside the Parkinson residence...

Lewis Parkinson is hiding behind the huge corner sofa downstairs in one of the back rooms. Much like Renato earlier, he has now become the victim of peer pressure and been bullied into watching a horror movie. He has given up trying to show off and appear macho in front of his companion. At present, he's way too scared to think about acting brave. Shielding his sight from the events taking place on the television, Lewis feels nauseous. Reacting quite the opposite, the dark-haired emo girl seems to be loving the terrifying scenes of blood, screams and horror. This new resident in the Parkinson household is Jesse's teenage daughter and her name is Eve.

Eve looks for a moment at Lewis cowering behind the sofa and laughs, then turns her attention back to the fifty-two-inch television screen, its surround-sound system blaring sound into the room. Her eyes remain dark, an air of secrecy hidden deep within them.

Onscreen, an actress screams out in agony, as blood squirts uncontrollably from what remains of her leg, the limb hacked off by the axe-wielding man who has chased her through the forest. She cries out for help from anyone who might be able to save her, but with no one coming to her rescue her screams become more desperate and lifelike. Lewis raises his head for a moment. Eve seems to be getting a deep internal thrill and satisfaction from this horrific and gory scene. His stomach turning, Lewis ducks back down. He can't keep his mouth shut any longer. "Nar, I'm not having this," he says. "That's fucking ill shit, Eve. How can you not feel sick watching that?"

Laughing, Eve replies, "Don't be a mard arse, Lewis." She begins howling with laughter. "Awww does the baby need protecting? Is the mean man making you poop your pants? I think Freddie or Terence would do a better job of watching this with me than you are. Shall I get one of their nappies for you, Lew?" Seeming satisfied with her taunting ways she says, "It's only a film –chill out."

"Shut up, Eve! I swear, man, it's fucked up. How do people even come up with that sick shit?"

"Easy. I could recreate that. Actually, I could write a way more horrific scene. Shall we create one now, Lew?" Suddenly she leans over the top of the sofa and shouts, "Boo!"

Lewis yells out with fear. Once he realises that it isn't the man on the screen coming to grab him, he says, "Behave, Eve."

Softening slightly, Eve says, "Come here – I'll protect you."

She lifts up the blanket resting on her shoulders and gestures for him to join her under it on the sofa. Not needing a written invitation, Lewis jumps straight under. Eve is wearing nothing but a tiny black vest top and silk shorts, the majority of her flesh revealed. Lewis instantly becomes aroused at being so close to her almost naked physique. Placing his head on her chest, Lewis peers up at her. She's engrossed in the film once more, and maybe she too is becoming aroused, but he can't tell whether that's to do with him or what she's watching on screen.

Once the actress takes her final breath and passes over to the afterlife, Eve, biting her lip, looks down at Lewis. The pair lock eyes. The silence says it all, oozing sexual tension. Shuffling down the sofa, they both now lie on their sides, face to face. Grinning, Eve seems ready for whatever comes next. Suddenly, she leans in and kisses Lewis. Receiving her soft lips, and with an erection growing inside his boxer shorts, he runs his fingers up her thighs. Continuing to stroke past the outside of her buttock, he gently tickles his way up her torso. Eventually reaching her slim neck, Lewis cups Eve's face in his hand, then gently twists her hair through his fingers. Thrusting himself on her physique, Lewis is keen to place himself inside of Eve. Moaning with gratification, Eve whispers into Lewis's ear, "Are you ready to hand over your soul to me?"

Trapped in the moment, Lewis is ready to agree to anything she wants if it means he can release the sexual frustration that's building up inside of him. Without so much as a second thought, he whispers into her ear, "Yes. Anything you want is yours."

"Right answer," she says.

He doesn't have time to process that her eyes have turned black, and it doesn't register that all is not as it seems.

CHAPTER NINE

Your Soul is Mine

Upstairs six-week-old baby Hope is sleeping peacefully in her room. The little girl's room has been decorated with an adorable princess theme. Hanging on the main wall is a string of beautiful handcrafted personalised patchwork bunting. In one of the corners stands a collection of all the wonderful gifts family members and friends purchased to celebrate her arrival into the world. In contrast to her four brothers' rooms, Hope's room is filled with over-the-top girlie items. This tiny girl is the light which the Parkinson family needed. Without her, each member, both big and small, at some point would have sunk into a cycle of hopelessness and depression due to their huge loss.

But right at this moment, baby Hope's room is being taken over by an energy which is far from angelic. Deep black shadows lurk in each corner of the room. Standing on the shelves are perfectly aligned rows of hand-crafted ceramic dolls, their eyes wide open. Each doll has matted blonde or brown tight curly hair and wears a uniquely designed dark and very unflattering dress. Scruffy and coated in dust, the worthless dolls have been in the Parkinson family for a very long time, passed down from generation to generation.

The head of one of the dolls twitches. It tilts to the side as cracks appear on her face. Taken over by something impure, the creepy creation stares intently at baby Hope and drops forward, landing in the cot. From the moment it makes contact, this simple white wooden piece of furniture instantly loses all purity. The netted drapes hanging over the side of the cot have turned black. A breeze develops, quickly building into a gust of wind that blows the drapes. This unannounced energy swirling around the room brushes past the princess-themed mobile hanging above the cot, setting off the melody built into the toy. The children's nursey rhyme plays slowly, sounding eerie and out of tune.

Completely unaware of the events taking place, Hope is sleeping deeply. A thick grey mist slowly seeps through the cracks surrounding the door. As the rhyming tune from the cot mobile stops, an ominous humming begins to build. Embedded deep within the room, the deceitful mist commences its attack, slowly seeping inside the cot. Surrounding Hope, the tainted mist wraps securely around her tiny physique, sinking deep into her pores and taking over her body and thoughts.

The evil manifestation complete, the Dark Empress herself finally arrives. It's Jezebel, and she's here to collect Hope. This malevolent sadistic entity is equipped and ready to unleash her evil supremacies amongst the universe. Her time is now, she's ready to claim what is hers and rule. She has carefully plotted and schemed with her chosen one by her side. Jezebel and Eve's demonic empire will be created using the souls of the young and vulnerable. The broken ones.

Standing in the corner of the room, her head low, Jezebel stares through the gap down the middle of her hair at the latest addition to her empire. She's ready to absorb the section of Hope's soul that will soon be surrendered.

As she steps forward, a sinister thick black substance is smeared across the floor everywhere she lands. Jezebel opens her mouth, the humming turning into singing. Instantly, the sinister black liquid gushes out and trickles down her chin. She slowly makes her way towards the cot, dragging one grey wounded foot in front of the other.

"Ring a' Ring o' Roses – your soul is mine. Ring a' Ring o' Roses – you've been chosen for the dark side."

The calculated words of the melody embed deep within Hope's mind. This devious energy sets about attacking her internally, taking over sections of her DNA. As soon as Jezebel arrives at the cot, the mist binding Hope's body slowly begins to release her. As it drifts away from her features, what it reveals is distressing. She no longer looks as though she belongs to the human race.

Jezebel places her hand on Hope's face. With black razor-sharp nails, this grey neglected body part oozes the same thick black substance from the deep rips in the skin.

"Ring a' Ring o' Roses – your soul is mine. Ring a' Ring o' Roses – welcome to the dark side."

The final word has been spoken. The transition is now complete. Hope's lips turn from pink to grey and cracks appear around her mouth. A thick black substance develops and begins trickling down her tiny chin. Once this devious shade takes over, her eyelids suddenly shoot open. No longer blue, her eyes have now become a true likeness of her new owner. Jezebel appears in the reflection of her eyes, which are now – jet-black! This baby girl's appearance is horrific. Basking in the euphoria she feels, embracing the power she possesses, Jezebel reaches out and holds her newest addition. And, with her coarse grey tongue, she begins to ingest the black substance seeping from the rips in Hope's skin. Instantly, their DNA becomes one. Without a sound, this baby girl has accepted her fate. Content with events that have taken place, Jezebel whispers, *"Non temere di me..."*

No sooner has this corrupt whisper travelled directly into Hope's ear than the curtains open unaided. Perched on the window ledge, shimmering next to the darkness of the night, is Jezebel's evil accomplice, the Raven. This strong oversized bird is riddled with evil. Her blood-red eyes glow against her jet-black silky, thick feathers. A disturbing thick bloody substance drips from her eye sockets and rolls down her feathers. The bird stares intently through the window at the events unfolding in Hope's room.

Jezebel slowly raises her head then gives it a sudden twitch and the window flings open, almost coming off its hinges. Stretching out her thick wings, in flies the Raven. She lands on Jezebel's shoulder and stares at the demonic empire's newest addition.

Content, proud and ready to implement the next step, Jezebel once again licks the black liquid oozing from the wounds upon Hope's face. The Raven joins in, pecking at the sinister substance.

Baby Hope is now tainted. She no longer belongs to the human race. Her soul has surrendered, now owned by two of the most powerful inhumane forms.

Across the hall, completely unaware of the goings on in her daughter's room, Alice is having a nightmare. Wrestling with the covers, she's soaking wet with sweat. Tossing and turning, she begins shouting in her sleep, "No, please, no!"

Alice gasps loudly and puts her hands around her throat. Her face turns bright red as she struggles to breathe. With one final huge intake of oxygen, Alice manages to break free and throws herself forward. At the end of her bed, two bright red demonic eyes are staring at her. Alice screams. No sooner has the cry left her mouth, the owner of those eyes throws herself on Alice.

Closing her eyes, Alice screams, "What do you want from me?!"

No response. Alice remains stiff, locked by fear. The silence continues and Alice bravely opens her eyes. A woman with grey skin and black hair hanging down either side of her face stands at the side of her bed. The two lock eyes.

The dark woman opens her mouth and a thick black substance travels down her chin. *"Morirai presto,"* she intones.

"What, do you want?" Alice says, her voice trembling.

The dark entity says nothing, merely tilts her head. Turning, she slowly drags her feet and makes her way back to the bottom of the bedframe. Still stiff and unable to move, Alice is powerless to do anything as her arms are suddenly stretched out and pulled over her head. Her legs are pulled in the same manner and restrained at the foot of the bed. Crying out in pain, Alice screams, "Please – why are you doing this?"

Screwing up her face, Alice feels a burning sensation on her wrist. Slowly the words *'they are mine'* appear. Tears begin to fall rapidly down her face. The dark woman twitches her head. Alice's arms and legs are instantly released. Grabbing her wrist, Alice reads the words. Her heart is racing. She has never felt this scared in all her life. Cowering, Alice looks to the demonic entity at the foot of her bed.

Desperate for answers she whispers, "Who are yours?"

Saying nothing, the entity charges at Alice.

Screaming, Alice throws herself forward.

As if waking from a dream, suddenly she is safe. She is in one piece. Soaking wet from head to toe with sweat, Alice reaches for the lamp at the side of her bed. She turns it on and looks at her wrist. Thankfully, there's nothing there. Leaning across to Jesse she tucks herself into his arm and whispers, "Jesse, I had a bad dream."

With his back to Alice, Jesse says nothing. His eyes snap open. They are jet-black. A huge smirk appears on his face.

CHAPTER TEN

The Hunt is On!

The Metropolitan Police Headquarters deals with undercover projects, gangs, drugs, murder and all the top-end crimes in Greater London. The huge building, with its spotless windows, stands sturdy, the official policing badge proudly placed on the exterior wall. New Scotland Yard holds secrets of all kinds.

Inside, the aircon is flowing at maximum capacity to keep the staff from overheating on this hot summer day. Rushing through the door, late as always, is Detective Chief Superintendent John Terry. Wearing a deep grey suit, and with his full-ish head of blonde hair, this friendly, unassuming figure has a smile on his face. He greets his colleagues in a mischievous manner. DCS Terry is old school. He doesn't adhere to the rules, he makes the rules adhere to him. Over the years, his quick wit and charm has saved him from many a tricky situation, including almost having his authority stripped and being placed on restricted duties. Many question his position, but this loveable, eccentric member of the force cannot be replaced. He has won accolades and praise for his impressive arrest record which includes multiple undercover assignments. As he has matured, his attention span has become somewhat shorter and he is easily distracted. Even though his work pace has slowed down over the years, the force just wouldn't be the same without DCS Terry.

Making his way to the reception area, he places his newspaper to the side as he scans his ID at the reception desk.

"'Ello, Mags. How's it going, beautiful?"

Sixty-two-year-old Margaret, one of the Metropolitan's longstanding receptionists for the past thirty years, is the only reason DCS Terry doesn't head straight to the lift and actually follows the signing in procedure. In the past he had tried to slip past the front desk without signing in, but this strong, "take-no-crap" woman had a job to do and no one was going to jeopardise it. Margaret had instantly pulled him back with a stern look that he knew not to challenge. Forced to adhere to the rules, rebellious DCS Terry always ensured it was worth his while by flirting with her. Fed up as it's too hot to be stuck indoors all day, Margaret replies morosely, "Morning, Tez."

DCS Terry formulates a cheeky reply that he hopes will make her smile: "You know it's not too late to book them one-way tickets, Mags. Me and you dump the ball and chains we've got and run away... What do you say? You going to finally take me up on my offer? I've only been asking the past, what... twenty years or so...?"

With a slight smirk she replies, "Tell you what, if I'm still alive, try me in another twenty."

"Ha, you know how to keep a man wanting more. Treat them mean, keep them keen. I know your game. After all these years I think I'm finally onto you." He laughs as he picks up his newspaper and makes his way towards the lift, calling back over his shoulder, "One day, Mags, one day."

"In your dreams, Tez!" she calls back.

DCS Terry walks out of the lift onto the tenth floor. The mint-green walls make the corridors seem longer than they are. The energy circulating around this section of the building is the opposite to the reception area. In fact, it's so quiet you can hear each squeak from DCS Terry's shoes, along with his heavy breathing as he's walking at a faster pace than usual. The tenth floor consists of two average-sized boardrooms and a third that's of a larger capacity, toilets and a modern kitchen. This soundproof section of the building is used to conduct matters that require confidential handling. Access is given to authorized personnel only. The vast majority of heated conferences regarding current high-end crime issues take place here.

DCS Terry taps on the wooden door and waits a brief moment before entering the boardroom with his head held low. He instantly sees Chief Inspector Lamont. He's wearing a deep blue suit with a crisp white shirt and ruby red tie. This man has a powerful presence and his style is immaculate as always. Standing proudly and centre stage, he's looking towards the door as DCS Terry walks through. With a slight smirk Lamont says, "Ah, morning DCS Terry. What a surprise – late as always, I see. Well, we're glad you could make it."

"Yeah, morning everyone sorry for my delay—"

Interrupting, Chief Inspector Lamont continues, "We're just starting now anyway, so you haven't missed much. Your seat's up front with me."

Seated in their designated places, each attendee possesses a matching collated bundle of papers. Taking his seat, DCS Terry begins indifferently flicking through the bundle. He loves his work, but he can't get his head around the paperwork trail that's required these days.

The meeting starts with a review of the agenda, but, due to the sensitive nature of the pending case before them, before any real discussion can get underway each member of staff must sign a confidentially agreement.

Clearly enjoying the authority which he has over the room, Chief Inspector Lamont says, "So, has everyone signed their agreements? If you're questioning whether you should indeed sign this document, then I'm sorry to say, you'll need to be reassigned. My advice to those of you who are struggling with this is to get out now and don't bother wasting my time or your own."

No sooner have the words left his mouth, then the attendees begin looking at one another. The newer additions who haven't worked with Chief Inspector Lamont before are confused as to whether he's being serious or not. But he doesn't retract his words, and, slowly realising this isn't a joke, they each sign the document before raising their hands and saying, "Yes, sir."

Continuing, Chief Inspector Lamont says, "Brilliant – full house it is, then!" Clapping his hands together he continues, "Right – now that that's out of the way, please refer to the paperwork in front of you. You'll find written statements and various interviews... etcetera, etcetera."

Watching Chief Inspector Lamont like a hawk, DCS Terry observes as he makes his way to the table next to where he sits. Present on the table are multiple piles of additional paperwork. Each pile is laid out in a precise and perfect order.

Grabbing one of the piles of papers, Chief Inspector Lamont continues, "What we have here are all the images taken. Any photographic evidence and still imagery from video footage. The real juicy stuff. Now, Joanna, be a doll and pass these evidence bundles to everyone." When Joanna, who doesn't appreciate the "doll" reference, doesn't instantly jump from her seat as soon as her name's called, Chief Inspector Lamont's tone becomes somewhat degrading. He says, "Earth to Joanna! Come on – let's not waste any more time."

Chief Inspector Lamont's Personal Assistant Joanna has the patience of a saint. Rising from her seat she responds, "Yes, sir. Sorry sir." And, without any hesitation she does as she has been told and begins handing out the additional bundles. The front page of each packet is plain white with black policing banners across the top. In the centre, in huge bold print, it reads – *Private & Confidential – Operation Bee Sting*. No sooner have the bundles been placed in front of them than each member begins eagerly skimming through the sheets of paper. The room becomes quiet, the atmosphere tense as they flick through the pages, absorbing the confidential information.

The newest members of the group are keen, excited and nervous, all at the same time. For some of them this is their first big case and the practicalities of what is expected of them when it comes to going above and beyond the call of duty is now more real than ever. After swearing the British Police Oath, they are required to stretch to extreme lengths. They must ensure they remain on high alert, ready for the unexpected. The attendees, from various police force departments, all have different skills, roles and serving lengths, but, this doesn't matter as each of them has demonstrated greatness and has proven their worth in some way or another, resulting in an invitation to this conference to become part of this case. Their job is clear, but far from simple. They're responsible for getting Britain's most dangerous and calculated criminals off the streets and placing them into custody. And their next target is Matthew Honey.

"Okay, so let's begin now that everyone is present…"

Resembling a child that's just been told off, DCS Terry says, "Sorry."

Ignoring Terry's apology, Chief Inspector Lamont continues, "Let's get to the main reason why we're all here today – *Operation Bee Sting*." He presses the button on the remote in his hand.

"This is something I've been working closely with some of you on for a while now. But, for those of you who are unfamiliar with this case, I'll give you the quick brief." Pressing the button once more, the clip changes, "First, we have our suspected perp, Matthew Honey, arrested on suspicion of killing his wife, Lauren Honey, and in connection to the disappearance of his daughter, Evelyn Jade Honey. He's currently on conditional bail. I'm not sure how, but the Crown seem to think he isn't a risk to society and that it's not in the public's interest to put him away - in their words, 'we don't have any real evidence.' I think this is a load of total B.S and, I don't back this decision one bit but, who am I after all my years on the Force?" Shaking his head, he continues, "Anyway, Matthew Honey is suspected of arranging the killing of his wife in a hit and run around four years ago. Lauren Honey, victim number one." Pressing the button again this now flicks to an image of Lauren. "Initially, we wrote this off as an unfortunate accident. We now suspect that this was all part of Honey's plan."

From the back of the room, a new attendee speaks up, "Sir, if you don't mind, pardon my interruption, but I'm sure I read somewhere in disclosure that Matthew Honey actually asked us to reopen the case because no one was ever made accountable for this."

"Yes – that he did. Let me ask you this PC…"

"Blackwood, sir."

"PC Blackwood. Okay, do you know how the mind of a criminal works?"

"Erm, I studied criminology for around four years, so I'd like to think I understand it to a certain degree, yes."

"Okay, so let's do some role play."

Appearing nervous, PC Blackwood hesitantly replies, "Erm, sure…"

"So, let's say you got someone to commit a murder for you – but, you knew there was a very slight chance that you could get caught out." Making his way around the huge boardroom table Chief Inspector Lamont says, "Now, to cover up your own tracks would you not plead your innocence to the world and act as though you're cooperating with everyone to the highest form? And, even go above and beyond, but – and this is the best bit, not actually push anything you're suggesting? All this in the hope that, if you ever do find yourself in a pickle and actually get caught out, you could say, 'Oh, excuse me, officer of the law, but why would I be cooperative and request for this to be investigated further if it was me that killed my wife? Are you following me PC Blackwood?"

"Erm, yes, Chief Inspector Lamont, sir."

Walking closer to PC Blackwood and almost standing behind him he carries on, "So, that being said, only you know that the trail is stone cold. There's no car, no perp, you have a perfect alibi and supportive witnesses – not only this, a location where all of the CCTV cameras are just slightly out of sight… I mean, I could carry on at how precisely planned this crime was…"

Twiddling his pen between his fingers and sweating slightly, PC Blackwood nervously replies, "Well, yes, I agree when you put it like that, I suppose it's extremely possible, sir."

"Okay, so would it be safe to say that this potential suspected perp with his own sick mind may have been trying to cover his almost clean tracks before we came knocking once more?"

"Yes, Chief Inspector Lamont, sir."

"Right, then, so what do you say, PC Blackwood, shall we get back to it?"

"Yes, Chief Inspector Lamont. Sorry, sir."

"Actually, does anyone else have anything they wish to share with the group before I carry on?" There is a deafening silence as the attendees regard one another uncomfortably around the table. PC Blackwood now has his head down and is sinking into his bundle of documents.

"Okay, so, as I was saying, Lauren Honey, victim number one. Tragic hit and run. Investigation was closed but the perpetrator was never found. We now believe Honey wanted revenge on his wife because he suspected she was having an affair. And also that he wanted her out the picture for his own financial gain. We're not one hundred percent on this, but we're slowly building our case and piecing bits together."

He presses the button once more and the screen flashes to a picture of Evelyn Jade Honey. "Now, this is where it gets confusing. We need to somehow link this messy murder puzzle together. This is sixteen-year-old Evelyn Jade Honey, victim number two. Matthew and Lauren Honey's child. Disappeared we believe around eight to ten months ago, maybe longer. Body never found. Evelyn's disappearance only came to light when her concerned family members and school teachers reported strange events. They also alerted authorities that she was missing. In particular Christina Hart, who is Lauren Honey's twin sister. Christina's daughter Melissa Hart has also made allegations regarding Evelyn's state before she went missing. Not only this, we managed to obtain a report from the Head Teacher of her school. Each of her teachers, at different times, have all mentioned strange incidents involving Evelyn Jade Honey, all of which happened during the days leading up to her disappearance. We now believe these were cries for help."

As Chief Inspector Lamont makes his way around the boardroom, DCS Terry is observing the room, and taking mental notes as he evaluates the level of engagement of each officer in regard to this case. Much like Lamont, he only wants 'A type' players on his team. He wants Matthew Honey to pay for the terrible things he has done to his innocent family. And so, he desires a fully pledged squad. A group that's eager and hungry to solve this crime and get justice for the two women who have been presumably murdered at the hands of this man. The man who should have been their protector. The same man who, in his eyes, completely abused his position and preyed on these vulnerable females. DCS Terry has now made it his mission to ensure that Matthew Honey pays for the crimes he has committed. Content with what he's seeing, DCS Terry sits back as he watches Chief Inspector Lamont drop the biggest bombshell, "Now, you may see our discussion as a little far-fetched, and you may believe Matthew Honey is innocent and question why, what, how and when, and so on, but, the truth of the matter is, and what concerns us most out of this whole case is that Evelyn's dad, Matthew Honey, never actually reported his daughter as missing."

The newest members in the room appear shocked as their eyes widen. The sceptical members are now utterly baffled by the words Chief Inspector Lamont has spoken.

"Exactly…! I know what some of you are thinking, what sort of parent wouldn't report their child missing?" He pauses, but not long enough to actually give anyone a chance to answer his question. "Yes, a guilty one! That's who…"

Looking around the room at the shocked faces, DCS Terry is content with the reaction of their chosen attendees. He smiles as the sceptics within the room now appear to be open to the opposing view. Scanning around the table DCS Terry suddenly sees PC Lola Hollingworth nervously raising her hand. Her hand trembles slightly. Once given the nod by Chief Inspector Lamont, she speaks. "Sorry for jumping in, sir. As shocking as that is, and please take this the right way, I'm somewhat intrigued."

He recognizes the young woman with the raised hand from a previous case. Chief Inspector Lamont replies, "Okay. What about, PC Hollingworth?"

"Well, it says here, on page thirty-six, that Matthew Honey presented some form of CCTV evidence, but it doesn't say what the contents of this were, just that this was dismissed, and the USB stick was stored away. Can you elaborate on this at all?"

"Yes! Rightful question and a very good observation, PC Hollingworth."

PC Hollingworth's hands stop trembling and she appears relieved. Placing her arms back on the table, PC Hollingworth grabs her pen, ready to making notes. Making his way back to the front of the meeting room, Chief Inspector Lamont confidently continues, "It's a simple one to answer, something which many of you may not have thought about. Actually, let me ask you, PC Hollingworth – why would you think that we would dismiss any potential CCTV footage we were presented with from this man?"

"In all honesty, sir, I'm truly unsure."

"That's okay. Does anyone else in the room have a suggestion as to why we may have dismissed this internal potential evidence? PC Blackwood, do you maybe have an opinion on this?"

"No Chief Inspector Lamont sir."

"Okay, so not one person in the room can tell me why we may potentially dismiss any form of video evidence that Matthew Honey may present us with. DCS Terry, what about you?"

"Well, of course I know why."

"Enlighten us."

"It's obviously because he's a film maker isn't it?"

"Yes! It's exactly that! And that's why you're a Detective Super, isn't it, Tez? No flies on this man. Matthew Honey is a professional film maker by trade. The footage he provided regarding supernatural activity and possession was laughable and nuts. He'd clearly produced this footage using his film making talents. Matthew Honey didn't know how to cover his tracks regarding his daughter. This time, he didn't have an alibi, any witnesses or even any explanation as to why he didn't report her missing. And yet, he rocks up with CCTV footage of hauntings in the night." Chief Inspector Lamont appears to be amused. Shaking his head, he continues, "So, this time, a broken and less confident Matthew Honey clearly panicked and for whatever reason he set about making a creative cover up film. Honestly, it's laughable. Maybe one day after you help me put him behind bars I'll dig it out of storage and let you watch the show." Scratching his head and rolling his eyes, Chief Inspector Lamont continues, "So, PC Hollingworth, does that answer your question?"

"Yes, it certainly does. It didn't even enter my thoughts, but yes, it makes perfect sense…" With a teacher's pet smile, she continues, "Thank you very much for explaining this, sir."

As the meeting progresses, months of work is revisited in as much depth as possible. Statement after statement, exhibit after exhibit – the evidence is overwhelming and copious. Yes, the challenge is strenuous, but each attendee is ready! This chaotic twisted trail has each of them guessing. Some evidence seems to suggest that Matthew Honey could have performed these awful deadly crimes against his loved ones. And other facts lead to a trail that's almost stone cold, with complications and unlikely possibilities. With the room divided as to Matthew Honey's involvement, all the important areas have now been covered.

It has been a longer working day than normal for most of the officers, but the essentials have been highlighted and DCS Terry is content with everyone's contribution to the meeting. Now that they're each armed with a vast knowledge about *Operation Bee Sting*, he believes that they're ready to take on the challenge. With the clock ticking, everyone has finally been allocated a role and a designated partner for the duration of the investigation.

One extremely satisfied authority member in the room is DCS Terry. He has been partnered up with Detective Constable Maria Flores. Taking in her tanned complexion and deep brown eyes, DCS Terry admires her natural beauty. It must be her partial Mexican heritage that gives her skin tone that wonderful glow. But he will have to put his unprofessional ways to the back of his mind. DCS Terry and DC Flores have been assigned the most crucial task within the room. They must conduct full surveillance on Matthew Honey – not just throughout the working day, but full twenty-four-hour surveillance. Wherever Matthew goes, they must follow.

DC Flores walks across to her colleague with mounds of paperwork in her arms, her structure strong, her shoulders back and her head held high. This passionate career woman is extremely confident in her role within the Force and will not be messed with. Balancing the paperwork on her left arm, she puts out her right hand to DCS Terry, "A pleasure to be working with you on this, sir."

Attempting to go in for a hug, DCS Terry says, "So formal, Flores. Come here."

Instantly stepping back and pushing her superior away, DC Flores says, "Let's get something straight, this is purely a professional partnership. I know of your reputation." Placing her hand out once more, she continues, "Now, let's start again. A pleasure to be working with you DCS Terry."

With a slight smirk and mischievous eyes, DCS Terry loves nothing more than a challenge. He has been here before, he's one hundred percent confident that he will charm his way through the barrier she has built. For now, DCS Terry decides to play the game and make her believe she's in control. And so, acting like a gentleman, he shakes her hand and replies, "The pleasure is all mine, Flores."

CHAPTER ELEVEN

Loyalties

The glass doors rotate rapidly as people continually rush to enter the building, whilst those inside jump into the fast-paced door system in order to leave. Like in a daredevil game, each individual hesitates before entering for fear of getting hit in the head by the spinning metal frame. Eventually, seizing the millisecond opportunity, they bravely hop into their chosen gap.

Inside this magnificent building, the uniquely designed interior fixtures make a bold twenty-first-century statement. Each décor item is in a prestige condition. Not a speck of dust can be seen. The windows throughout the building are gleaming. It's a brand-new day and natural sunlight is radiating around this beautiful structure, creating warmth and an angelic glow. Marching his way towards the door, suited and booted in his shark grey suit, light grey shirt, jade green thick silk tie, and with his briefcase in hand, Matthew Honey proudly enters the impressive premises, of which he is the owner. He's smiling from ear to ear. Positioned in pride of place, the words "Honey Productions" hang on the wall behind the reception area. Making his way to the reception desk, Matthew's greeted by Daniel with his usual hyperactive tone, "Good morning, Matthew."

"Good morning, Daniel. How are you today?"

"I'm alright, well, I had a solid session last night and there was an after party so I'm a little worse for wear, fuzzy head and all that jazz. But as we know, Matthew, that's showbusiness for you."

"What are you like Daniel."

"You know I'm a social butterfly."

"Yeah, that you are, Daniel. I swear, the youth of today, you all baffle the brain cells out of me." Laughing, Daniel continues, "You could do with some loosening up in that suit of yours. Come on, shake that booty."

With a huge grin, Matthew replies, "Ha ha, no you're alright thanks. Think I'll pass on that one."

The front desk phone begins ringing. Relived, Matthew can't help but feel that he's literally just been saved by the bell.

"Good morning Honey Productions Daniel speaking."

Smiling and turning his back to Daniel, Matthew heads to the centre of the reception area. Standing still with his briefcase in his hand, he absorbs the perfect ambience of the building. His empire, his pride and joy, his lifeline. Breathing deeply, he can feel the clean air filling his lungs to their maximum capacity before he breathes out. Matthew remains solely in the moment. Seeing the bodies of his employees and clients rushing around the building gives him a great internal satisfaction. As each person passes him they nod their head and bid Matthew "Good morning" before continuing to go about their day.

As he blinks his eyes and zones out, the movements of others begin to slow down. The people around him move at a snail's pace before eventually coming to a halt. It's as if time itself has frozen. Confused and in a daze, Matthew's breathing becomes heavy. He feels as if he's about to faint. Suddenly, deep within his mind, he hears the sound of sweet orchestral music, which gradually gets louder. This beautifully composed masterpiece relaxes him slightly, soothing his thoughts. Remaining in a trance-like state, raising both his arms, Matthew begins conducting the music he hears with his hands. Waving his briefcase in time with the symphony, he's truly appreciating and embracing the peacefulness he now feels.

The bodies of those surrounding him are no longer frozen. Like a ballroom dance, they've slowly drifted together and are now hand in hand with one another. Moving in time with the gentle melody that's playing, Matthew's employees and clients in sync with one another glide around him as he remains stationary in the middle of the reception area.

Gracefully conducting the music, Matthew's wrapped solely in the moment. As the brass instruments initiate and begin complementing this piece, the sweet sound of cellos, clarinets, harps and violins come back in. As more instruments sound in concert the symphony becomes louder and Matthew's sense of euphoria grows. No sooner has his smile begun to develop at this dreamlike musical masterpiece, his eyelids flicker and they gently open.

There lies the truth. Like a smack to the face, a hideous and horrific reality presents itself before him. He doesn't have a briefcase in his hand, he isn't wearing a grey suit with a jade-green tie. In fact, he's holding an almost empty bottle of vodka and is wearing the same black ripped jeans, faded dirty black t-shirt, leather jacket and beanie hat. There are no employees, no clients and the only other thing present with a heartbeat inside the building are the rats that have taken refuge in the walls and under the floors. Not only this, there's no sunlight. The building has been boarded up with thick brown wooden sheets. Matthew's pride and joy is no more! Honey Productions has gone into liquidation. Clients quickly rushed to sever all connections with Matthew Honey once the headlines hit and this empire, which was once strong, rapidly came crashing down. Like a domino effect, the personal tragedy that was out of Matthew's control had catastrophic consequences for his livelihood too. Remaining the owner of the building, he decided to keep hold of it until his innocence is eventually proven, in the hope of getting all his staff and clientele back and trading once more. This building, much like his home, is derelict.

Matthew is extremely intoxicated and is beginning to sway. Confused he turns around and says, "Daniel?"

There is no one there. Not a single reply. Drunken Matthew staggers around the empty, dark, dirty, cold reception area. Shouting and slurring his words he says, "Oh yeah, that's right, you all left me!" Swigging more of the vodka from the bottle, he scrunches his features as the liquid instantly warms his insides. "Me – Matthew Honey! Without me you would have all been nothing. Loyalties – pfft, there's no such thing."

Swaying across to the lift, he presses the button and waves the bottle around as he continues his rant, "I'll show you when I walk through them doors with my Evelyn Jade. And then what? You'll all feel the fools. Mark my words." As the lift dings and the glass doors open, before stepping inside, he shares his final thoughts with the empty reception area, "I'm Matthew Honey, you will never win against me."

Gulping down the remaining vodka, Matthew wipes his mouth before launching the bottle directly at one of the walls, where it smashes into thousands of pieces. He begins laughing hysterically at his destructive behaviour. Echoing around the empty reception area, this sinister cackle lingers even after the doors on the lift have closed.

Hearing both male and female voices rattling around his mind, Matthew gasps and jumps up. He had passed out drunk on the leather sofa in his office. Half asleep still but slowly coming around to the fact that he is no longer in the building alone, he grabs his pistol from the back pocket of his trousers in order to protect himself. Making his way towards the office door, he places his ear to the wood. The unknown voices sound serious and are getting closer. Stepping away from the door and panicking somewhat as there's nowhere to go, Matthew's aware that he's completely trapped inside his office. "Shit, shit, shit. Just stay calm, Matthew," he says quietly.

Pacing up and down and scratching his head, he has minutes, if not seconds, before the intruders come within metres of his location. Sobering up rapidly, Matthew places his back up against the wall and takes a deep breath in. Deciding to peer through the internal window which overlooks the huge office space where the voices are coming from, Matthew moves the blinds and scans the area.

Suddenly appearing from out of the distance are two presentable and well-groomed people. Gulping back the lump that has developed in the back of his throat, Matthew breathes deeply, places his pistol back down his trousers and opens the office door. The male and female haven't noticed him and so he shouts, "Can I help you? This is private property and you're currently trespassing."

They stop in their tracks and look across to where the voice has come from. Seeming surprised to see anyone inside this derelict building, the smartly dressed male says, "Ah, yes, I'm Detective Chief Superintendent John Terry and this is my colleague Detective Constable Maria Flores. We've received reports of unexplained noises along with a potential disturbance at this location. My colleague and I have been sent to check this out." Making their way across to Matthew, DCS Terry continues, "We noticed the building wasn't secure and so we entered to ensure that vandals hadn't broken in. Can I ask who you are, sir?"

"Yes, I'm Matthew, the owner of the building."

"Matthew?"

"Honey, why?"

"Just checking."

"I'm going to need to see some identification from you both."

"Sure, that's not a problem at all, Mr Honey."

Struggling slightly as he's reaches inside the internal pocket on his jacket, DCS Terry grabs his badge and shows it to Matthew. DC Flores does the same. "This is some building you've got here. Have you just bought it?" she asks.

"No, I'm currently having some family issues. But all will be resolved soon enough and then I can invest back into the building."

With a sympathetic tone DC Flores replies, "I'm sorry to hear that."

"Right! So, now that you know it's me in here I'd like to get on with my work, so can you please leave my premises."

DCS Terry responds, "Sure, not a problem. And, just so you know, we're always watching, day and night."

Trusting no one, and unimpressed with the words DCS Terry has just said, Matthew instantly bites back and says, "What do you mean by that?"

"I just mean, you know, we're always watching the area, making sure it's safe."

Remaining unconvinced even by this seemingly justifiable response, Matthew decides against digging any deeper. He wants these two untrustworthy authority members out of his building as fast as possible and so he simply replies, "Oh – okay."

"Okay, so now that we are aware that the building is secure we shall leave you to it. Thank you for your time, Mr Honey."

DCS Terry adds, "Yes, thank you for your hospitality." Slightly smirking he continues, "Sure I'll see you again at some point, Mr Honey."

Squinting his eyes, and with his head low, Matthew peers up at DCS Terry and this time he chooses not to reply to his goading words. A response isn't needed as Matthew's current facial expression says it all. Remaining cautious about this law enforcement officer, another potential enemy to add to his list, Matthew's instincts are telling him that something isn't quite right.

He follows them into the lift and they make their way down to the reception area, without anyone saying a word. Matthew watches as they both leave the building. He then locks the doors.

CHAPTER TWELVE

Has Anybody Seen My Daughter?

S itting at his desk with his head in his hands, Matthew feels as if his brain is swelling. It's pulsating, thumping repeatedly against his skull. He's developing a strong sense of nausea along with an intense pain that shoots through his eyeballs. Feeling unsure if he's strong enough to take on the challenge and find his daughter, Matthew is struggling to focus. He is in a very deprived and fragile state. Without a single molecule of alcohol inside his body, without his confidence juice, Matthew's depression and lack of self-worth has kicked in. He looks at his hands, which suddenly begin to tremble. His body is attempting to detox, whilst at the same time he is craving the next drink. Not only are his thoughts confused, his internal organs are also much the same.

Matthew's inner voice begins tormenting him with destructive and cruel words, telling him, screaming at him, that he needs more of the toxic substance. He begins searching the office, but all he finds is empty bottle after empty bottle. As if his body is punishing him, Matthew suddenly feels as though he has been hit by a bolt of lightning. His stomach begins to hurt. All of his internal organs, one by one, are cramping with great intensity. Curled over, he falls from his chair and vomits in the metal bin at the side of the desk. Wiping his mouth on his sleeve and pulling himself back up onto the chair, he has never felt so poorly. As the strength of the cramps continues to grow, each one contracts quicker than the last with every second that passes.

The strong, acid tang of the vomit takes over his taste buds. Matthew begins searching for anything he can eat or drink to remove this awful flavour burning through his oesophagus. He's even willing to settle for something non-alcoholic. Searching the drawers of his desk, he finds an old sweet shoved at the back. Without even thinking about the use by date, he unwraps it and shoves it in his mouth. Relived as the fruit juices take over, he closes his eyes and breathes deeply so he doesn't vomit.

"Mind over matter, Matthew, it's just mind over matter."

As he opens his eyes, he looks at the dusty picture frame on his desk. The image is of him, Lauren and Evelyn Jade. Picking this up, he wipes the dust and cobwebs off with his hand. As tears instantly form in his eyes, he says, "How did we get here?"

Kissing the image, his tears land upon the glass. Bringing this close to his chest, he speaks once more, "I will not let you down any longer. I will be the man I should have been. I will get our daughter back or I will die trying."

With his pep talk over, Matthew switches on his computer and gets to work. He downloads the most recent image of Eve from her social media account before she went missing, smiling as he reads the caption she wrote on the image: #nofilter. These words of truth begin warming his heart. Eve's such a naturally beautiful young girl, with her striking long golden hair flowing down her face. He sees his princess. This is exactly how he remembers her. Cropping the image and placing it against a black background, Matthew begins designing the text for his leaflets. In huge bold white letters, he types: "Have you seen my daughter? Please contact me on…" and he leaves his mobile number at the bottom.

Content with this simple yet effective leaflet, Matthew hits the save button and then print. As the leaflets print the pain continues to travel around his body. Unable to ignore it any longer, Matthew surrenders and goes on the hunt for any pain relief he might be able to find.

Holding his stomach and hunched over in a crippled state, he enters the kitchen area. Searching all the cupboards, he manages to locate the first aid box. Thankfully inside he finds a box containing strong pain killers. With his hands continuing to tremble from the alcohol withdrawal, he struggles to pop two of the tablets from out the packaging. No longer having patience, he bites through it and shoves two of the pills in his mouth. He then wraps his lips around the tap at the sink and swallows the pills in one go.

Slumping to the ground, all Matthew truly desires is an alcoholic drink. Just one drink. After all, that's not going to get him drunk, and really, how bad could one drink truly be? Without needing much convincing, Matthew lifts himself off the ground and heads back into his office to collect his leaflets.

Pulling up outside the entrance to his derelict looking building, his thoughts racing at a hundred miles per hour, Matthew releases a deep sigh. He knows this is it. There's no going back. His time is now!

He loads four boxes, that are sitting at the entry way, into the foot well of his car, grateful that he was able to transport it all downstairs with only two trips on the lift. Each one's filled with Matthew's distinctive leaflets. As he slowly drives towards the exit, Matthew reflects that, with the recent changes to his life, this gateway isn't so inviting anymore. The barrier which was once in place to protect the grounds has been completely ripped off. Stopping at the exit of the car park, Matthew glances out at the empty booth where Eric once sat. He's no longer greeted by his bright-eyed chirpy security guard. Saddened by this, Matthew closes his eyes for a moment.

Determined to win his life back, he's ready to face the unknown. He puts the car into gear and makes his way out of the car park, empowered by a strong sense of bravery. But as soon as he is driving down the road he quickly reverts to being nervous and unsure. Matthew's mind once again begins taunting him, feeding him words of destruction. He pulls up at the side of the road, his hands trembling. Once again he feels a huge bolt of pain shoots through his stomach. In excruciating agony, Matthew opens the car door and vomits on the pavement. He feels momentary relief as his body releases the acid that was building. Desperate to soothe his pain and satisfy his addiction, Matthew racks his brain to locate the quickest route to the off license. The only desire he has at present is to stop the nausea, the jitters and the agony he feels. But, whilst he's solely fixating on this, Matthew fails to notice the black minivan containing DCS Terry and DC Flores pulling out from a side road and following at a brief distance.

CHAPTER THIRTEEN

Let Me Help You

"What's that you've got, dear?" Dorothy asks, standing in the kitchen doorway.

Her back to the door, Alice jumps. She was obviously completely unaware that her mum was there watching her. Wiping her eyes, she quickly shoves the piece of paper she was reading into the drawer and replies, "Oh nothing – it's nothing."

"It doesn't look like nothing."

Alice wipes her face once more. Her cheeks turn a slight shade of pink. She wears a smile from ear to ear, but her eyes are sad, as if she is holding back the remainder of her tears. She makes her way to the cupboard and grabs their favourite mugs. Looking back at her mum, she says, "I'll make us both a nice hot drink. Yeah, a hot drink, that's just what we need right now."

Unluckily for Alice, her mother has uncanny intuition when it comes to her daughter. And, even though Alice is a mature adult, Dorothy doesn't for a millisecond believe her words. Remaining suspicious, whilst at the same time attempting to keep the peace, Dorothy smiles back and replies, "Sure, my dear, that will be lovely."

Dorothy walks over to her daughter, who's rustling around the kitchen, and as she's taking the milk out of the fridge she stops Alice in her tracks and holds her gently by the shoulders. Gazing at her precious girl with nothing but sheer admiration for her courageous strength, she begins tucking the lose strands of Alice's hair behind her ears as she says, "Do you remember that time when we went fishing with your uncle Tony?"

Alice laughs, sniffling a bit at the same time, and replies, "Yes."

"And you looked like you were struggling with your line, so I said, 'Alice, my dear, do you need any help?' And what did you say almost instantly?"

Alice smiles and rolls her eyes as she answers. "I said, 'I'm fine.'"

"Yep – 'I'm fine' is what you said. And then what happened?"

Trying her hardest to hold back a smirk Alice says, "I fell in the pond."

They both break out in huge grins as they relive this memory. Dorothy continues, "Yes, you fell in the pond. Now, what was the moral of the story, my dear?"

Alice hesitates, as if reluctant, then says, "It's okay to ask for help, or to accept help, from others."

"So, I'll ask you again – what was that you were reading?"

As the joyful memory fades, tears slowly begin to form in the corners of Alice's eyes, "It's just a letter, Mum. Honestly, I'm okay."

Unconvinced by Alice's attempt to hide her feelings and stay strong, Dorothy guides her towards the kitchen door and says, "Why don't you go and put your feet up with Hope, my love. Come on, while the children are in school. Lewis and Eve are at college. And, he who shall not be named is out I'll..."

Interrupting, Alice says, "Please don't start Mum."

"I'm not starting anything Alice." Looking at her daughter and seeing her physical appearance is deflated and her eyes have dark rings around them Dorothy surrenders. With her hands up, she says, "Okay, okay, While the kids are at school and college and *Jesse* is out, is that better?"

"Yes it is, thank you."

Holding Alice by her shoulders once more, Dorothy begins guiding her daughter out of the door.

"Good. Now, let me look after you. I'll finish cleaning up and make us both a cup of tea and a sandwich. How does that sound?"

"That'll be great, thanks, Mum."

"It's fine, that's what I'm here for. Now go and squeeze that precious baby girl of yours."

As soon as Alice leaves the room, Dorothy makes her way to the kitchen drawer and retrieves the piece of paper her daughter was trying to hide. Aware she's on limited time, she doesn't attempt to read the contents and shoves it inside her pocket for fear of getting caught. Just as she is about to place the tea bags in the mugs, she hears a high-pitched scream coming from the front room. Instantly dropping the mugs on the floor, Dorothy runs to her daughter's aid.

"Alice! Alice! What is it?"

Her baby in her arms, Alice is screaming, "No, God no! Please no! She's not breathing, Mum! Please do something! Help me, she's not breathing."

"Oh my goodness!" Frantic, Dorothy runs for the phone and calls the emergency services. "Ambulance, please! We have a six-week-old baby and she isn't breathing. Please hurry."

"Please try and stay calm for me. Do you know CPR?" says the operator.

"No – Alice, do you know CPR?"

Crying heavily, Alice replies, "No." Whispering to her daughter she says, "Come on, baby girl, everything is going to be alright. Hope – please – please – please don't leave me. I need you."

Dorothy's attention returns to the phone as the operator says, "I'm going to talk you through CPR until the paramedics arrive, okay?"

"Yes, anything, please hurry!"

"Right. Lie the baby on his or her back on a flat surface. Let me know when you've done this."

"Alice, you need to lay her down on a flat surface."

Alice brings Hope over and lays her down next to Dorothy.

"Okay, we've laid her down."

"Now, using two fingers in the centre of the chest just below the nipples, give thirty chest compressions rapidly. Try and be as gentle as you possibly can. I will count with you. Are you okay to do this for me?"

"Yes, I'm doing them now. Ten, eleven, twelve... Come on, Hope."

When Dorothy reaches thirty the operator continues, "Now that that's complete I need you to tilt the baby's head and lift the chin, then give two effective breaths directly into the mouth."

Dorothy does as she is instructed. "I've done it but she's still not breathing!" she says, panicking.

"Please just keep repeating the CPR procedure until the ambulance arrives. Continue to count your chest compressions and give effective breaths."

At the sound of approaching sirens, Alice runs straight out the front door to flag down the ambulance.

Now alone with baby Hope, Dorothy continues to give her CPR. Midway through, Dorothy loses the connection on the phone and the speaker begins blasting a fuzzy interference sound. Confused and frantic with worry Dorothy shouts, "Hello?! Hello?!"

But there is no reply. Feeling unready for the challenge she is now facing alone, Dorothy suddenly sees Hope's eyes flash open. She drops the phone and stares at her granddaughter in disbelief. All is not as it should be. Dorothy freezes. Hope's once pure eyes are jet-black! Not a trace of her natural blue shade or even a fraction of white can be seen. Her eyes are like gaping holes in her face. Without making a sound, Hope slowly turns her head to look directly at her grandmother. Dorothy throws herself back with force in sheer shock at this horrific image, banging her spine on the frame of the sofa. She gasps and shouts, "Hope!"

Closing her eyes, Dorothy prays that her mind is playing cruel tricks upon her. But when she opens them she sees that her prayers haven't changed a single thing. The truth is clear and the image before her is horrific!

As she stares in total shock at her granddaughter, a drop of black liquid appears in the corner of the baby's eye. It slowly descends Hope's cheek like a tear.

Overcome by fear, Dorothy unexplainably begins to choke. She gasps for air, coughing in an attempt to dislodge whatever is lodged inside her throat. But it doesn't work, and now her tongue begins to swell. Dorothy is struggling to breathe No matter how hard she tries to free herself, she is unable to catch her breath. Curled over, Dorothy falls onto her back. She's slowly giving up, surrendering to the powerful energy controlling her body.

In the distance, Dorothy hears a familiar nursey rhyme of playing: "Ring a' Ring o' Roses". Gradually getting louder, the eerie children's melody travels through Dorothy's ear drums, sinking deep into her mind. The haunting tune slows down with every second that passes until its final dulcet note sounds. A brief silence ensues.

Suddenly, an ear-piercing screech shoots directly through Dorothy's brain. Desperate to shield herself from the excruciating sound, Dorothy places her hands over her ears. But it's as if the sound is not coming from an outside source – as if it has already been embedded in the darkest depths of her mind. Growing weaker with every second that passes, Dorothy becomes more lifeless.

As the final molecules of oxygen drain from her body, Dorothy wheezes loudly. Lying rigid and flat on her back, she drifts in and out of consciousness for milliseconds at a time. Dorothy is very aware that at any given moment her life could end. She prays for a release. No sooner has she started to ask for help than, like a punishment for praying, her internal organs begin to shrivel as the blood and oxygen circulate no more. Protruding from her sockets, her eyes immediately turn bloodshot red. The internal pressure too much for her body to bear, Dorothy lies motionless.

Baby Hope's lips have turned grey. She's now a reflection of her new owner. Her existence has been claimed. This innocent baby girl no longer belongs to the human race. Captivated and cursed before her thoughts were her own, baby Hope has surrendered. The dark force at work has gained the newest member of her demonic empire. Staring directly at her dying grandmother, Hope smirks.

Suddenly, like an alarm, Alice's frantic voice is heard shouting "Hurry!" as she enters the house alongside the paramedics.

Content with the acceptance of her possession, the evil entity releases her hold over Dorothy and Hope. Turning her head once more, baby Hope slowly closes her eyes. Instantly, her skin tone resumes its normal rosy shade. The black substance is absorbed into her skin, as if it never existed. And Dorothy's body is freed from the shackles of this sadistic and possessive takeover.

Dorothy is slowly regaining consciousness. Her hands still placed around her throat, she suddenly feels the blood begin to pump through her heart and travel around her body once again. At the same time oxygen rapidly circulates in her system, and Dorothy feels her lungs expanding as they fill to maximum capacity.

"Quick, she's in here!" Alice shouts as she enters the front room.

She runs straight to her daughter, who is lying on the floor. The paramedics enter the room straight after Alice and kneel at the side of baby Hope, pushing Alice out of the way. Alice turns and looks over her shoulder, spotting Dorothy,

"Oh my goodness! Mum, Mum, are you okay?"

Unable to speak properly Dorothy mimes, "Yes. Help baby."

Alice gives the paramedics, who are armed with all the essential tools required to save this baby girl's life, the space they need. She rushes to her mum and kneels down at her side.

Having regained her composure and regulated breathing, Dorothy finally has ownership of her body once more. She's unsure whether to tell Alice and the paramedics what has just happened. Looking to her distraught daughter, Dorothy decides it's best to keep the truth to herself. Instead, gathering her strength, she does the only thing she truly desires and grabs her daughter. Holding her tightly in her arms, Dorothy places her head close to her heart. Clutching Alice as if this is the last time she's ever going to see her, Dorothy begins breathing in her daughter's sweet scent. Distraught, she closes her eyes as her tears drop one by one onto Alice's hair.

Across the way, the paramedics are doing everything they can to save Hope. Fearful of the unknown, but desperate to reassure Alice, Dorothy says, "Everything's going to be alright." Her voice is husky, her throat raw. Coughing and in a lot of pain, she's petrified not only by what has just happened, but by thoughts of what is yet to come. Closing her eyes, she whispers to Alice, "Shhh, my dear, I've got you. Mum's got you."

Seconds pass, though it feels as though time has stood still. Waiting for what feels like an eternity, Dorothy suddenly flinches as she sees Alice beginning to wretch. Alice's body then begins to sway.

"Mum, I feel like the room is spinning."

"Alice darling, I'm right here."

"Mum – please, help me everything's moving very, very slowly." Placing her hand to her head, Alice very faintly says, "Please make sure they save Hope. Mum, I think I'm going to..."

Interrupting, Dorothy pleads, "Alice, just stay with me."

Alice whispers, "Mum, I think I'm..." Slumping toward the floor, Alice passes out.

Powerless, Dorothy watches her daughter collapse.

Dorothy tries to shout out but her throat is still raw. She manages a feeble, "Alice! Please!" Then, looking to the paramedics: "Help me – she's not breathing."

One of the paramedics quickly goes to Alice. Checking her pulse, she says, "She's ok. She has just fainted. Lay her down safely and go and grab a cold compress and some water for when she comes back around."

Sobbing, Dorothy replies, "Okay."

Placing a pillow on the floor, she rests Alice's head on this. Slightly unsteady on her feet, but with the power of love for her daughter taking over her body, Dorothy goes to the kitchen and grabs the items. As she tenderly presses the cold compress against her daughter's head, Dorothy gently sobs. She strokes Alice's hair off her face. "Come on, Alice, please. Everything's going to be okay, I promise. Just please wake up."

As the medics continue to administer CPR, suddenly, through some miracle, Hope screeches and turns a bright shade of pink. She's breathing again.

"Alice, Alice, she's breathing," Dorothy tells her daughter. "She's alive. Please wake up. Alice, if you can hear me, Hope is okay."

As one of the medics tends to Hope, the other now makes her way across to Alice and takes her observations.

"Alice, can you hear me?"

Alice remains unresponsive.

"Alice, if you can hear me, my name's Tara. Can you make a noise for me, please?"

Suddenly, Alice groans.

"Alice, I'm here, my dear," Dorothy says. "Hope is okay. You're all going to be okay."

Looking to Dorothy, Tara says, "Please can you stay here for a moment with Alice? Keep pressing this on her head. I'm just going to get the stretcher out of the ambulance."

"Of course, I'll do anything. Just help her, please." Looking to her daughter with relief, she whispers, "See, I told you everything was going to be alright. I have you, my dear. I have you."

Making her way towards the door, Tara says, "Pete, I'm going to get the stretcher. If mum comes around shall we place both mum and baby on one together, or shall I get the incubator just in case?"

"Get the incubator. Don't want to take any risks. Mum's not stable enough yet."

"Okay, will do."

"We'll need to hook them both up to the vital signs monitor, too. Can you get them ready?"

As soon as she arrives back with the stretcher and the incubator Pete and Tara rush both mum and baby into the ambulance. Without any hesitation, Dorothy dives into the back of the ambulance. Still weak and in shock, Alice mumbles, "Mum, the boys, they need collecting from school. Lewis and Eve also need collecting from college."

Leaning over her daughter, Dorothy says, "Shhh, don't worry about them, I'll sort everyone out."

"Jesse, you need to tell Jesse."

"Yes, and Jesse. I'll let him know."

Alice whispers, "He'll be okay with the boys. Thank you for everything, Mum. I'll call you from the hospital."

"Shhhh… You get some rest. Don't worry about the boys, I'll check with Jesse or else I can take them. And, as for calling, don't you call me, I'll call to check on you two, okay my dear?"

"Okay."

Dorothy kisses her daughter then makes her way over to her granddaughter. She peers into the incubator at baby Hope. There's not a shade of grey in sight and not a spot of black upon her skin. Her eyes have resumed their normal shade. Baffled, and believing it all must have been a figment of her imagination due to stress and lack of sleep, Dorothy kisses Hope on the head once more and then gets down from the ambulance.

Teary eyed she says, "You take good care of my girls, please."

"We will, don't you worry," Pete replies as he hops into the driver's seat.

Standing at the back, Tara says, "Okay so we've got your details. Are we okay to put you as next of kin?"

"Yes, please do. Will someone be able to call me and let me know what ward they're on?"

"Erm, well, ideally if you ring the reception and give details they can provide this information. But, you may have to pass security first."

"That's not a problem. Okay, so I'll call in around an hour and see how they're getting on."

"Yeah, that's possibly your best bet."

Grabbing the paramedic, Dorothy holds her tightly in her arms. This professional has just saved her world from falling apart and she's more than grateful. Smiling, Tara hops into the back of the ambulance to take care of Alice and baby Hope for the duration of the journey to the hospital. Dorothy watches them drive off down the road. Once they are out of sight, Dorothy heads back inside the house and closes the door.

Resting her back on the windowpane next to the door, Dorothy tries to process what on earth has just happened. Caught up in her thoughts, she fails to notice the sudden change of ambience within the house until a tingle shoots down her spine. The hairs on her arms stand to attention, creating pimples on her skin. As the unnerving energy gains strength, Dorothy suddenly realises that she's no longer alone in the house. Feeling extremely vulnerable, she shouts, "Hello?!" Deep down she prays no one will answer.

She's being teased by entities unknown. No longer feeling brave, Dorothy rushes into the front room. Grabbing her belongings, she runs to the front door to let herself out – except she can't, because the door is unexplainably locked! No matter how hard she pulls down on the handle, Dorothy is unable to free herself. Panicking, Dorothy begins kicking the door and screams, "Help!"

As she heads towards one of the other doors, a strong gust of wind suddenly blows down the staircase and knocks Dorothy off her feet, causing her to fall and hit her head against the banister. With a split on her forehead, she curls up, unable to move.

As she lies on the floor quietly sobbing, blood drips from the gash on her head. She vomits on the floor. Her body convulses as she goes into shock. A pungent stench travels up her nostrils, awakening her senses. Dorothy feels an excruciating pain throughout her internal organs. Suddenly, Dorothy's body stops convulsing.

Drained of more than ninety percent of her life, Dorothy lies in a heap at the foot of the stairs. Her eyes are open wide. Her wounded, cracked skull now feels like a weight has been dropped on it from a great height. She throws up once more, the vomit dripping from the side of her mouth. Once again, she begins drifting in and out of consciousness. No longer in control of her own body, her eyes unexpectedly close shut as she whispers, "No…"

A thick grey mist develops and begins making its way down the staircase towards Dorothy. Reaching her battered body and wrapping tightly around her physique, the dark energy paralyses her. She can no longer even so much as wiggle her own fingertip. Empowered by this control, and with a grip that's getting stronger, the deceitful mist creates bonds around her entire being. Its formation complete, this possessive controlling manifestation calls for its owner. No sooner has the command been given than she arrives at the top of the staircase. There she is!

Her eyes closed and unconscious, Dorothy is completely unaware of the demonic entity which is only a few feet away from her. Jezebel slowly descends the staircase and walks towards Dorothy's paralysed body. Once there, she leans over Dorothy's prone form, reaching for the back of Dorothy's neck with her horrific razor-sharp nails. Pressing her nail deep into her flesh until she draws blood, Jezebel engraves an upside-down cross, making deep cuts through the layers of flesh. There is not so much as a flicker from Dorothy. Collecting the sinister black substance from one of her gaping wounds, Jezebel embeds it into the gash she has just created on Dorothy's neck. She smears the deceitful substance, mixing it with Dorothy's human blood. Content with the captivity of Dorothy's soul, and with her head low, she spits her black substance as she says, *"Mi temerai."* Leaning over, she continues, "Do you like to play games, Dorothy?"

Dorothy remains unresponsive, and Jezebel smirks. Her jet-black hair hangs heavy on either side of her face and the black substance gushes from her mouth as Jezebel speaks once more: "You have been marked. You have been warned. You will stay away. You will not win against me. They are mine; you will see. Stay out and I will let her live. Try to stop me and I will ensure that she dies. Her life or death is in your hands. You decide…"

CHAPTER FOURTEEN

You Know What to Do

Purity fills the air as the bells chime throughout the centre of Rochester. Standing strong with its sandy coloured bricks, the second oldest Cathedral in England is unique for many reasons. Its distinctive architectural construction is of the Normandy era. Rochester Cathedral also has a dark, gothic and medieval design throughout. It's breath-taking for all the right reasons. Many flock here to worship and celebrate whilst embracing the stunning historic exterior and interior as they become captivated with their surroundings. The energy circulating within this magnificent building is powerful. During the day, sunrays beam through the huge handcrafted stained-glass windows. Each colourful creation has a biblical meaning and helps to radiate warmth and a tranquil glow. With wooden benches placed all around the floor space, this immaculate cathedral is ready for the faithful who are in need of spiritual guidance or those who need to feel a spiritual connection through their faith.

At present, darkness has fallen. Even with the intimidation of the night, this blessed building remains secure and safe. The evening prayer service has just finished and there is only one attendee left inside. Familiar with the surroundings, Matthew kneels with his hands just above his head in the prayer position, deep in thought. Feeling as though he's surrounded and supported by the guidance of angels, Matthew embraces the non-judgemental environment, shedding a single tear. Closing his eyes, he sees a clear vision in his mind. This wonderful event which has chosen to surface is of his wife before her light went out. The days when life was simple. The days when life was worth living for the right reasons, the easy reasons. He sees Lauren standing at the alter inside Rochester Cathedral. She is wearing an elegant, silk, ivory, wedding gown. The material is hugging her body in all the right places. Staring at her, Matthew is in awe. He cannot believe his luck. Gazing at her beauty, Matthew sees Lauren's radiant smile beaming across at him. She looks just like an angel. Seeing the smile she wore once more, Matthew feels an intense burst of love. Yes, Lauren maybe deceased, but this will never stop his love for her.

Having been forced into the hardest challenges of his life, Matthew has spent a long time feeling as if the world has turned against him. After getting over his anger at the decision maker upstairs for apparently cursing him with this path, he has now found comfort in the power of prayer.

Believing he's alone, Matthew speaks. "Forgive me, Father, I have a selfish prayer. I don't know what to do. I ask you for guidance. Answers to the unknown. How can I continue to live freely when all that I had in this lifetime has very cruelly been taken away? My daughter – she is all that is me. My gift from you. All that is left of my wife. I ask you, I beg you, I implore you, please help me on this hunt. Please give me faith and instil strength in me, so that I know I can get her back and bring her home where she belongs."

He squeezes his eyes tightly together and breathes deeply. Before he has chance to continue with his prayer, Matthew hears a voice echoing from behind. "I know why you are here, Matthew."

Shocked, he turns and sees Reverend Andrew Read making his way towards him. Matthew hasn't seen Reverend Andrew for a long time. He has been busy with business and life changing tragedies, and the years have mounted up quickly. Although he enjoyed tonight's service, Matthew was certainly surprised to see Reverend Andrew conducting it, given that he is now beyond retirement age. Now just a few feet away, Matthew looks closely at Reverend Andrew's features. It's clear to see the years have caught up with him. His skin is sagging and coated with wrinkles. Not only this, his hair is the purest of white.

"It's been sometime since I last saw you, Matthew."

Paranoid that he might be judged for entering this house of God stinking of alcohol, Matthew nervously says, "Erm, I know I haven't been by it's just…"

"Matthew, after all these years, you should know by now that you don't have to explain yourself to me." Smiling, he continues, "I've known you since you were just a young boy. I'd like to think that you know me well enough to understand that I do not judge, my child."

"Of course."

"Matthew, you seem troubled and lost."

"I am, I really don't know where to go or who to turn to." Feeling isolated, Matthew hangs his head. "Did you hear about Lauren and my daughter Evelyn Jade?"

Putting his hands together, Reverend Andrew responds, "Yes. Matthew, I am sorry for your huge loss. Having bonded your love to Lauren all those years ago on your wedding day and having the ability to bless young Evelyn Jade at her christening, I truly feel a personal connection to your loss and continue to pray for you all. I think this is why I have been chosen."

"Chosen, for what?"

"All will reveal itself soon enough."

Confused, and feeling slightly uneasy, Matthew doesn't wish to press the matter any further. "Reverend Andrew, sorry, I'm… I… erm, shouldn't have overstayed my welcome. I just wanted to speak with the big man upstairs once everyone had left. I didn't know anyone would still be here, let alone you. I should probably just go."

"Matthew, it's okay, I was just in the sanctuary blowing out the candles. Please, don't be sorry, you're always welcome in this house, you know that, Matthew. Here, you are safe."

"Thank you, Reverend."

Sitting next to Matthew on the solid dark varnished wooden seat, Reverend Andrew continues, "Guidance you ask for, then guidance you shall receive."

"Thank you, Reverend, but I'm not sure you can help me with this one."

"Matthew, of course I can help you. I am one of the Lord's chosen messengers. I'm here to bring guidance from within. My purpose is to empower those who need it directly from the Lord himself."

"You can give me guidance from the big man upstairs?"

"I certainly can. As I said, I have been chosen."

Sceptical, Matthew questions Reverend Andrew further. "Chosen? Okay, if you have been chosen, then you will know exactly why I'm here?"

"Yes, you seek the return of a loved one. You seek the love from her heart."

Laughing slightly, he says, "Okay, Reverend, lucky guess."

"I promise you, I have been chosen Matthew. I have a message for you. Do you wish to receive it?"

"Right now, I'll try anything."

"This young girl, you will receive."

"What?! I'll get her back?"

"Matthew, be calm."

"Calm! Reverend, how can I be calm when you've just said that?"

"Matthew, please listen to me."

"Yes, you've got my attention. Believe me, I'm listening."

"You need to understand that the challenge is hard. Your path is unclear. You are fighting evil – this is serious. Tainted trails will blacken your vision and darken your sight. Your mind will be taunted, your soul will be teased indefinitely. You must remain strong." Looking to Matthew and raising his eyebrows in disapproval he says, "The alcohol, Matthew. You must sacrifice this."

Breathing deeply, Matthew knows the reverend speaks the truth, but it doesn't make the thought process any easier. Alcohol is his confidence juice. It's what was going to get him through the challenge of finding his daughter. He closes his eyes and inhales, then opens them and replies, "Okay, Reverend. I'll do it."

"You're not doing it for me. You're doing it for your chosen path. You can't have a weak mind. You will lose. They're too strong for you."

"I know. I promise, Reverend, I will stop."

"I don't think you truly understand just how huge this is, Matthew."

"I think I do. Reverend, I just want my daughter back."

"That's all well and good, but, Matthew, as I've said, you're fighting evil. The darkness within."

"Yes, believe me, she's already almost killed me once and has ensured my life was destroyed in the hope I'd probably kill myself. Oh, believe me, I know exactly what I'm facing."

"You must listen to me, Matthew, when I say that whatever your result, you must accept this path… your destiny…" Reverend Andrew reaches out and separates Matthew's hands, which were still tightly held together. He places a solid gold cross into them. "This cross has been blessed and soaked in holy water. When the time is right, you will know what to do. Stab their hearts with this, but—"

"Huh? Hang about, stab their hearts… I can't… I won't…"

"You must. It's the only way."

"But… Rev…"

"Matthew, listen to me: you must stab their cold hearts. But this is the important part. These hearts, they are not the hearts which you may think. These hearts do not beat."

"What does that even mean?"

"It means, when the time is right, you will know. Only then will you be free to live your life with her pure soul. The soul of the young. Matthew, only you can save us from the evil that lies within. Only you can break the sadistic entities that will destroy our world as we know it. Since our first meeting all those years ago when you were just a little boy, I knew. I knew that this was and always has been your destiny. Please, trust me."

Matthew is gobsmacked. He's trying to process the Reverend's words. Sobering up rapidly, he gulps and looks to the cross in his hand. "I..."

"You need say no more. Matthew, just know that we are always with you. The Lord is always with you. You will need us for this journey, but tune in no matter where you are – guidance will always be given. Good luck, Matthew, and please be extremely careful. The darkness is more powerful than you think."

Getting up, Reverend Andrew says nothing more and walks back the way he came.

"But... Rev... I..."

Matthew watches as he disappears into the darkness of the cathedral. Confused and unsure whether he even possesses the ability to stab his daughter's heart, Matthew attempts to process what has just happened.

Unable to come up with any answers, Matthews places the cross inside the pocket of his jacket and decides to finish his prayer. "I take my selfish prayer back. I pray for the weak, I pray for the strong, I pray for the young, I pray for the old, I pray for the wealthy, I pray for the poor, I pray for every individual soul, I pray for the world. If it is my destiny to fight evil and free the world, then that is what I will do, or I will hand myself to the afterlife for failure of my purpose." He stands. Just as he's about to walk up the aisle, Matthew turns a final time and says, "Purpose accepted."

CHAPTER FIFTEEN

Catch Us if You Can

It's just past midnight and the Parkinson residence is uncomfortably silent. Every room has been taken over by the darkness of the night. The only sound that can be heard is the echoing of ticks and tocks from the clocks throughout the house. One by one, each of the clock hands begins to slow down as the time pieces gradually fall out of sync with one another. Every tick and every tock now produces a flat tone. Suddenly, all the clocks tick their final tock. Time officially stands still. The hour, minute and second hands move no more. Not a twitch or a tiny flicker can be seen. The clocks are completely frozen.

A suppressive, gloomy energy is travelling at a rapid rate throughout the family home, its overbearing vibration permeating the walls of this sturdy structure. Positioned on the wall next to the front door, the thermostat begins to change, the digital numbers descending. The temperature throughout the house plummets from cosy to way below zero.

The unexpected shift in the climate of this family home brings with it a dark formation that is ready to intimidate the purest and most vulnerable residents. The relentless mist returns and begins to thicken, establishing itself throughout the downstairs of the Parkinson family home. Taking over the space, it travels up the dining room walls. Cracks slowly begin to appear in the glass of each of the family pictures hanging there. Not content with simply damaging the Parkinson family shrine, the unforeseen force strengthens. And suddenly, every picture frame is launched across the room, crashing on the floor and smashing into thousands of pieces.

Developing rapidly, the dark grey mist flows up the stairs at the command of its mistress. Its heading towards the bedrooms of young Lewis, Freddie, Terence and Rupert, who are all tucked up and asleep in their beds. The boys have been left in the sole care of Jesse whilst their mum and sister are recovering in hospital. Believing they will be cared for, the Parkinson boys are actually more vulnerable than ever.

The evil entities that have been welcomed into their home are now ready to claim what they believe is rightfully theirs. The Parkinson boys don't stand a chance against these powerful, calculated and sadistic individuals. They have fed on their vulnerability and gained strength. Now Jezebel and her evil accomplice are free to implant their malicious DNA inside their tiny minds.

Inside Terence and Rupert's room, the dark blue walls absorb the darkness. Shadows lurk in each corner. On the ceiling and glowing brightly are decorative stars, both big and small, illuminated against the darkness. Toys are scattered everywhere across the floor.

On one side of the room, Terence is sleeping inside his plastic Ferrari racing car bed. Across the way, in his less cool white wooden bed, lies Rupert. He's too big for a cot, and yet too little for a single bed. Mirroring his brother, Rupert is dreaming peacefully.

The two young boys are completely unaware of the evil intrusion that has forced its way into their bedroom. They are blissfully ignorant of the horrific truth that awaits them. Terence and Rupert are soon to receive their fate. A tainted new pathway has been mapped out for both of them. Having instantly gained ownership of Hope Parkinson, the dark forces at play now focus their attention on the two Parkinson boys, who are next in line.

Alice Parkinson has been tricked into welcoming two of the most sadistic, impure and powerful entities into her broken family home and she's about to pay the ultimate price. Ready to destroy this family and take what she believes is hers, Jezebel is content with her chosen souls.

Continuing its deceitful takeover, the intimidating mist seeps through the cracks of the bedroom doorway. As this intrusive energy enters the boys' room, the temperature has already registered at below zero. As the boys' chests rise and fall in their sleep, each tiny exhalation can be seen in the cold air. Rapidly gaining force, the energy creates a huge gust of wind that sets the curtains blowing, their metal loops aggressively clinking as they are almost ripped off the pole. The mist thickens, wrapping tightly around the mess throughout the room and travelling up the walls.

With full reign over the room, the dark force is ready to implement its next calculated steps. It has been sent to absorb and capture the souls of the young! Separating, half of it ventures across to Terence and the other half to Rupert. It latches onto the framework of their beds, forces its way inside the boy's bedsheets. Starting with their toes, like glue it attaches itself securely to their feet and travels up each of their tiny physiques. Instantly, the boys' nerves react to the sub-zero temperature of the mist as it sends pins and needles throughout their little bodies, the hairs on their arms and legs standing to attention.

A fearful expression appears on Terence's face. It's clear that he's no longer feeling the joy that comes with sweet dreams. Grasping onto his DNA and travelling through his blood cells, this possessive energy continues its intrusion and takes over his mind. Terence's thoughts are now plunged into the darkest depths, where all his worst fears live. The innocent four-year-old boy scrunches up his face, struggling against the violation to his body. The mist now wraps around his throat, without enough force to choke him. Desperately fighting against the evil, Terence's body is rejecting the unknown entity attacking his DNA. As this ultimate genetic battle continues, Terence's tiny body begins to tremble, then convulse violently. Suddenly, his mind unwillingly surrenders. The captivity is complete. The human DNA inside his body is now tainted. Terence abruptly shakes one final time before landing flat back on the bed.

Across the room, two-year-old Rupert, much like his older brother, has also been restrained by the mist. Sharing the same fearful expression, both boys begin to whimper. Lost deep inside their unconscious minds, they've gone from skipping in the park and swinging high into the sky to suddenly landing inside the darkest depths of an unknown forest.

Finding himself alone, Terence shouts, "Mummy…?"

In the deafening silence, the only sound this terrified little boy can hear is the echo of his own voice. In a state of panic, Terence bravely shouts once more, "Where you, Mummy? I scared."

But still he gets no reply. Tears stream from his eyes. Unsure whether to run or stay where he is, innocent Terence has never experienced confusion like this. Going into protection mode, the voice inside his head tells him to remain still. But, being the brave and inquisitive little boy that he is, Terence decides to wipe his face, gather his strength and courageously walk out into the trees.

Sobbing to himself, he once again shouts, "Mummy…?"

This time, he hears, "Yes, my child…"

Relieved, Terence looks around. Seeing no one he again shouts, "Mummy, where you?"

Echoing from the distance, the voice reappears, except this time, it doesn't at all sound like his mummy. With a dulcet tone, the evil that has locked him deep within says, "I'm right here, my child."

Confused and uncertain, this time trying not to draw attention to his location, Terence whispers, "Mummy…?"

The little boy stands perfectly still. The only part of Terence that is now moving are his eyes as he desperately searches the dark forest for his mummy. Squinting, he sees a black figure appear from the distance and elegantly make its way towards him. Within a millisecond of engaging in eye contact with this figure, Terence's little heart starts uncontrollably beating.

The unfamiliar voice once again speaks. "Do you… like… to play games… Terence?"

Scared out of his mind, Terence doesn't reply. His little legs begin to wobble and his knees bang together. Levitating, the evil entity feeds from his fear and, like a magnetic pull, is drawn directly towards Terence. Suddenly flashing right up in front of his face, the horrific entity with blood red eyes says, *"Non temere di me..."*

Alone in another area of the eerie forest, two-year-old Rupert is curled up on the earthy ground with his eyes closed, crying inconsolably. Surrounded by autumnal leaves, he's sucking his thumb. Feeling scared and vulnerable, this innocent little boy shouts, "Ma mam...?"

He gets no reply.

Down the hallway in his bedroom, eight-year-old Freddie is fast asleep in his bed. His features matching the earlier expression of his younger siblings, he rapidly becomes distressed and begins battling with his bedsheets. The deceitful mist drifts across to Freddie, weaving itself around his body and creating its restrictive bonds. The evil energy wraps around Freddie's throat, drawing tighter with every millisecond. As Freddie is older, his level of awareness is more profound than his younger brothers. He instantly feels a sharp tingling sensation traveling throughout his entire body, like tiny bolts of electricity surging through his veins.

Freddie quietly whimpers in his sleep, his mind and body fighting this uninvited energy. Desperate to relieve himself from the discomfort and pain, he throws his body forward and forcefully wakes himself up. But, as he opens his eyes, he sees that all is not as it should be. He's surrounded only by darkness. Expecting to be inside his bedroom, and aware that he isn't, Freddie's mind has gone into overdrive. He is unaware that he's been cunningly locked deep within the darkest depths of his own mind. In a bid to get help Freddie shouts, "Lewis?!"

But, he gets no reply. The only sound he can hear is his own voice echoing in the distance. Each of the boys are now stuck inside their greatest fears. They have no one to turn to and nowhere to hide. The boys are more vulnerable than ever. And, that's just the way the Jezebel wants them to be.

Jezebel stands at the foot of Rupert's bed in her true horrific form, peering at the young boy. It is time. She is ready to collect his soul. She reaches out, dripping the thick black substance on his bedsheets. Her grey neglected hand hovers over his face, just millimetres away from his innocent and pure skin. She stares at him with her blood red eyes, hanging her head low. Jezebel is ready! In her dulcet tone which is unknown to the human world she sings, "Ring a' Ring o' Roses – your soul is mine. Ring a' Ring o' Roses – you've been chosen for the dark side."

Weakened and without any resistance, Rupert's unprotected soul receives its fate. Embracing the words of the possession, his tiny mind doesn't attempt to fight. Almost immediately, his skin tone changes. Content with the development and Rupert's acceptance, Jezebel makes her way across the room to Terence.

Arriving at the side of Terence's bed, Jezebel tilts her head, staring at her next target. A proud, deceitful smirk forms upon her features. Her lips part slightly and the thick black substance gushes from her mouth and rolls down her chin. Terence has already absorbed the possession. He now lies stiff. A black line forms around his neck as the mist descents. Terence no longer appears as though he conforms to the human race. His eyes are jet-black, bottomless gaping holes to be feared. His veins are no longer blue, his blood is no longer red, his skin tone an inhuman grey. This young boy is now a mirror reflection of his new mistress, their DNA intertwined.

The thick black substance now has full control over the boys. Surrounded by a pool of the nauseating sticky liquid, Terence and Rupert lie motionless. Standing in the middle of the room, Jezebel raises her arms with euphoria as the final transition takes place. Suddenly, Terence shoots up from his pillow. Almost instantly, Rupert mirrors this action. The bedsheets rise with them as the boys levitate from their beds.

In her new demonic form, Eve stands in the corner of Freddie's room, staring at him as he restlessly sleeps. Her eyes are gaping holes peering through the gap in her hair, which hangs symmetrically down either side of her face. Freddie struggles in his sleep as the mist thickens and surrounds him. Eve slowly makes her way towards the young boy, humming with every step. The humming turns into singing, and as she reaches the side of the bed, her words become clear: "Ring a' Ring o' Roses – your soul is—"

Just as she is about to continue with her possessive rhyme, Freddie suddenly wakes, breaking free from the entrapment. His head shoots up from the pillow and he throws himself forward, instantly screams when he sees the terrifying figure standing at the side of his bed.

Lewis is in a derelict room. He looks up to see his mum swinging from the ceiling, a rope secured tightly around her neck. As her eyes begin bulging from their sockets, Lewis attempts to run to her aid...

Lewis suddenly wakes, sweating from head to toe. His hands are shaking and his heart is pounding heavily against his chest. In a daze, Lewis places his head in his hands. Suddenly he hears the screams of his younger brother. Still half asleep, Lewis goes into autopilot. He throws himself out of the bed and rushes towards his brother's room, tripping over his own feet. In a complete panic, Lewis fails to notice the drastic change that has taken place within the household. Hearing Freddie's desperate pleas, Lewis bursts into the room shouting, "Freddie! Freddie! What's wrong, mate?"

As soon as he sees his young sibling, he realises something isn't right. Freddie is sat upright, screaming as he stares into the corner at what appears to be nothing. Walking towards the bed to comfort him, Lewis says, "It's okay, mate. You can stop screaming now." But still Freddie continues.

Holding his brother securely and on high alert, Lewis hears a creak coming from the hallway. His cries getting louder, Freddie raises his arm and points to the doorway. A sudden gust of wind forcefully slams the bedroom door shut. Lewis squeezes his brother, feeling utterly freaked out. Not wanting to pass his anxiety to Freddie, Lewis says, "It's okay, mate. Come on, let's go and stay in my room."

He wraps Freddie up in his sheets and scoops him out of the bed. As Lewis turns around to leave, he freezes. Freddie immediately starts bawling again. A tall dark figure stands at the door. A creaking sound draws Lewis's attention to the window. Making her way from the darkest corner of the room is a smaller version of the dark entity. As Freddie continues to yell, the tall figure looks to him and mimes, "Shhh..."

Freddie is now unable to make a sound. Horrified at the events unfolding, Lewis whispers to himself, "It's just a nightmare. Any minute now you're going to wake up." Closing his eyes, he continues to reassure himself desperately, "Any minute now. Any minute."

Opening them once more he sees the truth: nothing has changed. Except that the two horrifying figures are now closer, trapping Lewis and Freddie inside the room. They both begin to sing, "Ring a' Ring o' Roses – your souls are ours. Ring a' Ring o' Roses – you've been chosen for the dark side."

Slowly placing one foot in front of the other, the smaller figure makes her way towards the boys. With every step, she continues to sing the creepy rhyme. The boys are frozen stiff with fear. Lewis opens his mouth to cry out but realises that, just like Freddie, he can't make a sound.

Freddie's head slumps back and his eyes begin to turn black. Looking to his younger brother and repulsed by the horrific transformation, Lewis instantly releases Freddie from his grip and scurries back onto the bed. He's overwhelmed by fear, staring in complete disbelief at what is taking place before his eyes. The two demonic figures are at the side of the bed, continuing to sing the nursery rhyme. Lewis can see them breathing in his brother's soul. Suddenly, the tall figure lunges at Lewis.

Gasping for oxygen, his throat dry, Lewis throws himself forward. He's soaking wet from head to toe... and is unexplainably back inside his own bed. Uncertain of what has just happened, Lewis looks around the room and sees that all is as it should be. It's the early hours of the morning and the sun has started to make a slight appearance. Relived, Lewis lies back on his pillow. Holding his hand on his chest and feeling his heart beating rapidly, he's unsure if it was all just a bad dream. Desiring clarification that all is as it should be, Lewis makes his way to Freddie's room. He turns the handle quietly so as not to disturb his little brother and peers only his head through the gap he's created. In the meagre daylight in Freddie's room, Lewis can see his little brother. Thankfully, he's still sleeping in his bed. Smiling, Lewis closes the door, scratches his head, and yawning, he makes his way back to his bedroom.

As soon as he enters, he jumps. Sat up straight in his bed and staring directly at him is Eve. His adrenaline spikes and his heart once again begins beating rapidly.

"Nah, Eve, for fuck's sake, man – you scared the shit out of me."

"Awwww, I'm sorry, baby. I just wondered where you'd gone, that's all."

Lewis climbs back into bed, and Eve opens up her arms to him. As soon as he's comfy she whispers, *"Mi temono..."*

CHAPTER SIXTEEN

Secrets!

Dorothy wakes up shouting, "No! No! No! Alice!"

She sits up on the leather sofa she had passed out on, dripping from head to toe with sweat. Gasping for air, she frantically looks around. She sees that, thankfully, everything is the way she had left it, with the lamp still glowing in the corner of the room. Relieved that she's free from the terrifying nightmare, she places her head in her hands, letting it sink in that it was just a bad dream.

But the horrific vision she has just seen continues to taunt her. Unable to cope, she sobs and breathes deeply. Feeling her lungs stretch as they expand to their maximum capacity, Dorothy begins to panic. Her heartrate sets off pulsating faster and faster. Continuing to breathe deeply in through her nose and slowly out through her mouth, she closes her eyes, placing her hands on her chest. Embracing the inner sense of calm which she now feels, Dorothy lies back. But no sooner has her head hit the arm of the sofa than the horrifying image which woke her from her sleep suddenly flashes at the forefront of her mind once more.

Dark and unrecognisable, the room in this vision is cold and unnerving. Thrown on the floor on its side is an old dark wooden chair. Hanging from the ceiling is a thick, coarse rope. Dorothy sees her only child, Alice, swinging from the rope which is tightly wrapped around her neck, her lifeless body hanging heavy. The pressure from the strangulation has taken its toll on her body and Alice's lips have turned a deep shade of blue. Her eyes are wide open and bulging from their sockets.

Shaking her head to remove the sickening vision and throwing herself off the sofa, Dorothy trips over the empty wine bottles surrounding it. They clink loudly, falling one after the other in a domino effect and rolling across the wooden floor. Dorothy rushes and grabs the phone. Tapping redial, she calls the direct line for the ward where Alice is currently recovering with baby Hope in Wythenshawe Hospital.

"Hello, ward seven, Mavis speaking."

"Hello, hi…" says Dorothy, out of breath. "Erm, Mavis, can you check on my daughter for me, please?"

"Sorry, who's calling?"

"Oh, yeah, sorry. Erm, it's me." Still trying to catch her breath, she continues, "Dorothy Davies, I'm… Alice Parkinson's mum."

"Just let me check that." Dorothy can hear Mavis tapping on a keyboard. "Yes, I can see you called earlier. We have you down as next of kin. What is it you would like to know?"

"Please, I'm desperate – can you just go and check on her for me? I know it's late, but I'm really worried."

There is a slight pause.

Choosing to seize the moment, Dorothy pleads, "Mavis, I'm not sure if you have children, but Alice is my only child. The baby she's with, Hope, she's my only granddaughter. I just want to know they're okay, that's all." As the silence continues, Dorothy tries one final time, "I would come on the ward myself but it's the early hours of the morning and you won't allow me to do that. Or, actually, is it okay if I come and check?"

"Okay, I'll check for you. Just this once thou—"

"Thank you so much!" Dorothy interrupts.

"Well, don't think about ringing every night, because next time the answer, I assure you, will be no."

"I promise, thank you, thank you, thank you, Mavis, I'm truly very grateful."

"Sure, just hold the line. I'll be back in a minute."

Dorothy waits anxiously. It feels as if Mavis is gone for an eternity, when in reality it's only a short amount of time before she picks the phone back up and says, "Hi, Dorothy?"

"Yes."

"Both mother and baby are doing fine. I've checked in and they're sleeping. Machines are all good, observations seem okay. You can stop worrying now and get some sleep yourself. You're no good to them exhausted."

Breathing once more at the relief she feels from Mavis's words, Dorothy replies, "Wonderful news. Thank you so much, Mavis. I'm sorry for intruding at such an early hour."

"No problem. But as I said, it's just a one-off."

"I know. I'm very grateful."

Ending the call, Dorothy goes to the kitchen. She places the phone on the side and walks across to the wine rack. Grabbing an unopened expensive bottle of her favourite red wine, she pours herself a large serving. Releasing a huge sigh, Dorothy looks to the glass and appears deep in thought. Then, without any further hesitation, she throws half of its contents to the back of her throat. Shaking her head, this strong woman is attempting to work out how her life has journeyed into such a temperamental and unnerving place. Having lived a life where everything goes her way, she suddenly feels as if, at any given moment, she's about to lose it all! And, to top it off, she's unable to stop it from happening. She's almost ready to surrender and admit herself to the mental health unit for assessment over the sickening image that's taunting her. The only thing stopping Dorothy is the mere fact that her daughter isn't swinging from a rope – she's very much alive and highly vulnerable herself.

Dorothy has never experienced anything like this. The disturbing events currently taking place leave her baffled. However, Dorothy is aware of one thing, one definite fact: her life has only become difficult since the day Jesse and Eve arrived. But right now, locked by fear and the potential risk of losing her daughter and grandchildren, Dorothy feels she has no choice but to remain silent. How can she even begin to explain the supernatural events that have been taking place? With no one to turn to, Dorothy's unsure how she's going to break free and help her family. Alongside this worry, unannounced, and making an appearance whenever it so desires, a loud and very present inner voice has begun interrupting her thoughts daily. Like an alarm bell with a broken snooze button, this voice is persistently sounding off at her. A deep gut feeling has also developed. This inner instinct is sending strong warning signals to her brain. Combined, these two powerful spiritual senses are telling her that something just isn't right, and the whole focus is on her daughter!

With the events of the previous night playing through her mind, Dorothy throws the rest of the contents in the glass to the back of her throat. Another image flashes in her mind, this time of her granddaughter. In this disturbing vision, baby Hope is grey, her black eyes empty of a soul. This snapshot sends shivers down Dorothy's spine. Her stomach turns and she rushes to the kitchen sink, where she throws up the alcohol which she has just guzzled.

Acid burns the back of her throat and a bitter sick taste circulates around her mouth. Tired and deflated, she slumps to the floor. Catching her breath and holding back the further surge of vomit which is trying to escape from her body, Dorothy closes her eyes. She tries to remain in control but her mouth begins to water, the persistent burning ball of acid forcing its way up once more. Unable to hold it down any longer, Dorothy's mouth fills with a thick lump of sick. Immobile on the ground, Dorothy has no choice other than to throw up on the floor. She wipes her mouth, and as the strong scent of vomit travels up her nose she gags. Tears form in Dorothy's eyes and her head begins to spin.

Desperate to get up and clean the sick from off the floor, Dorothy attempts to lift herself but almost instantly falls back down. Talking out loud she sternly says, "Right, get up, you silly woman." Her mini pep talk over, again, she tries to lift herself, and again, she fails. Tilting her head back against the cupboard door, Dorothy pleads internally. Relaxing and controlling her mind using meditation techniques, Dorothy manages to slow down her heartrate. She knows the challenge ahead is going to be strenuous, and in order to get help, she's aware that she needs facts, evidence and some form of trail. At present, Dorothy hasn't got so much as a slight inclination as to where she should begin. From nowhere, her desperate pleas and prayers are answered. Dorothy sees a clear image. She has remembered something that might help. Something that could result in the first step being taken.

Renewing her efforts, this time embodied with motivation she slowly drags herself up with the support of the kitchen unit. Using the tiny amount of upper body strength that she has, Dorothy regains her footing. She cleans up the aftermath of the puke attack and, hobbling slightly, makes her way out of the kitchen and heads to the coatrack in the hallway. Flicking the light on, she frantically searches for the jacket she wore earlier. After pulling out every item and throwing them on the floor, Dorothy remembers it was actually a cardigan she was wearing.

Making her way back to the lounge, she finds the garment hanging over the arm of the sofa. She reaches inside the pocket and pulls out a scrunched-up ball of paper. It's the letter she retrieved from Alice's kitchen drawer. The same letter Alice was attempting to conceal from her earlier. The piece of lined paper has lots of wear and tear upon it. It's clear that it has been retained for some time. Opening it slowly so as not to rip the fragile paper, Dorothy almost instantly works out what this is. She immediately recognises the perfect cursive handwriting in blue ink. Her daughter has been keeping a huge secret. The biggest secret of all. On this piece of paper is her son-in-law Phil Parkinson's suicide note. Dorothy had no idea. Her hand over her mouth in shock, she's unsure whether to read the entire contents. She battles with the voices inside her head – one side of her brain is telling her to leave this well alone, whilst the other is persuading her that at least glancing over this personal message is the right thing to do. And so, before she talks herself out of it, Dorothy starts to read…

Dearest Alice and children,

I truly don't know what to say. This is the hardest choice of my life to date. To live or to die… How can I make this decision? How does life get to a point where you're worth more financially dead than alive? This cruel cycle of life, the game of cat and mouse, so to speak. And now I've been caught in the trap.

You're all my world, but that isn't enough to get us out of the mess I have created. It's time for me to be the man you need and rectify my life-long mistakes. One crooked path after another.

You deserve the world, my queen, and that is what I'm going to give you. But it comes at a price, and unfortunately the price which has to be paid… is me!

I apologise that I'm not going to be around to watch our children grow.

I apologise that I'm not going to be around to support you as a wife and a mother.

I apologise that I'm not going to be around to hold you at night, stroking your hair until you fall asleep, telling you everything will be okay. I truly apologise.

As long as I am alive, my queen, it's not going to be okay. I didn't want it to come to this but here we are.

I have to make this right. It's time for me to look after my family, and if that means me not being around, then I will sacrifice myself and leave the family unit. Just please remember, no matter what, I'm doing this for love! Promise me you won't forget I'm doing this with a full heart for you all. No longer will you, or our children, suffer.

All I ask in exchange for my life is that you please allow me one wish… You don't have to, but can you read between the lines and call our one and only daughter Hope Eva Lia Parkinson.

You won't understand right now, but one day you will see, it's going to be okay.

I apologise for the pain, my queen, to you, our princes, and our princess. Please know, I'm doing this for us. Our debts are too high, life will be too sad. The money from the insurers and the pay-outs you will receive should be around £1.2 million, so please invest this wisely and look after yourself and our babies.

One more thing: I'm going to stage this as though I've been fishing. You need to pretend fishing was a hobby of mine or the insurance companies won't pay out. It must look like an accidental death. Burn this letter so it's never found. I promise no one will find my body, the rocks will conceal me. They'll never be able to perform an autopsy. No one will know. I love you always. I'm sorry it has to be this way!

Until we meet again, my queen.
Forever Your King, Phil

Dorothy sits in silence. She's struggling to process what she has just read. Placing her hand to her head, she's overwhelmed with a mass of sadness. Her daughter has been carrying this huge secret single-handedly. Not only does this make her heart break even more – Dorothy is now confused as to why Alice didn't confide in her. After all, she is her mum. She truly believed that they were close enough to support one another through anything.

CHAPTER SEVENTEEN

Getting Warmer

"Excuse me, sir, have you seen this girl? She's my daughter." With the sun blaring and sweat dripping off his head, Matthew's desperately attempting to hand out his leaflets. Much to his despair and frustration, he's being completely ignored. Walking around the streets of Chester, he's being judged and looked upon by passers-by as if he's some sort of escaped mental patient due to his current desperate demeanour and scruffy attire. Matthew's not having much luck encouraging the public to engage with him. Unfamiliar with his accent and too scared to make eye contact, most people are avoiding Matthew at all costs. Without wanting to be rude and trying to retain a slight air of politeness, each person looks at their phone or at the floor. With no idea where to start, and the only potential clue being a diary with the words "up north" written inside of it, Matthew is making his way up the United Kingdom. And, no matter the hour, be it day or night, he perseveres.

Stopping at every town, village and city that he possibly can, he has been franticly searching street after street, wearing the same heavy-duty boots. This sturdy footwear wasn't designed for long-distance walking, and so each footstep grows more painful as Matthew distributes leaflet after leaflet. Determined not to give up, he pushes through the pain barrier. He wishes he was made out of steel, but since this unfortunately is not the case, the wear and tear upon his body from the boots is now taking its toll. He is hobbling slightly, and huge blisters are growing on the backs of his feet as the boots rub relentlessly. He has remained sober in order to stay focused, but now Matthew finds himself yearning for an alcoholic beverage to numb his senses. But with Reverend Andrew's words fresh in his mind, Matthew is fully aware that he must remain sober. Breathing deeply, Matthew refuses to allow the pain to stop him as he bravely pushes on.

Without one phone call from or sighting of Eve, this ongoing hunt is at times deflating, but Matthew won't give up. After all, his daughter is the only person he has left to live for in the world. And, not only this, she's also the only person who can clear his tainted name. He continues with his desperate pleas as he attempts to hand out the next leaflet, "Excuse me, miss... Miss... Have you seen my..." Turning to the next person again he says, "Sir... Sir... Can you help m..."

But again, the sad reality is he's continually being ignored. He has been at this for the past six hours straight. Accepting defeat for the moment, Matthew makes his way across to the benches facing the river. Placing the leaflets on a wooden bench, he sits beside them and reaches inside his pocket and pulls out his cigarette box. This is yet another habit he has taken up of late. He lights a cigarette and inhales a draw that takes almost half of the cigarette away. Exhaling the smoke, he places his head in his hands and attempts to soothe his mind and release the frustration he feels.

Matthew can't understand why people are being so unhelpful. Even before his life was shattered into millions of pieces, at the height of his success, he still made time to help anyone he could. It didn't matter what your position was in life, whether you were the CEO of a multimillion-pound company or homeless and sleeping and living in the same clothes every day – Matthew would always ensure that he gave every individual the same dedication of time and most certainly the same amount of respect. The way he saw it, we all have beating hearts and we enter the world the same way, we just chose different pathways. Although now, after the degrading way he's being treated by the public, he is questioning this.

Looking out to the river, he sees the ducks, swans and boats bobbing up and down on the water and passing by with ease. Embracing the tranquillity of the calming water and nature's true beauty, Matthew quietly takes in the view.

"She's pretty, who is she?"

Snapped out of his daydream, Matthew looks to his left and sees a girl no older than five or six years of age. Her hair is in pigtails and she's wearing a stripy t-shirt with denim dungarees. She is sitting next to him with one of his leaflets in her hand. Looking around for her parents, Matthew sees that her mum is standing not too far away from them on the phone. She's having a rather heated conversation with whoever is on the other end.

"That's my daddy. They shout all the time."

Confused, Matthew says, "Huh?"

"Mummy is talking to my daddy. They don't like each other."

Saddened by her words, Matthew replies, "I'm sorry to hear that, sweetie."

"It's okay, I don't like daddy too, he's mean and smells like boys. Yuck!" she says chirpily.

Laughing at her innocence, but sad that she has that opinion of her father at such a young age, Matthew says, "So, what's the one thing you do like about mummy and daddy?"

"Well, my mummy makes me giggle a lot because she's silly and she takes good care of me. And my daddy, erm, well, erm, when I stay in his house, he sings me a song. It's special because my daddy puts my name in it. You want to hear it?"

"Sure."

"So it goes... Darcey is my baby girl princess, she's my one and only princess, she's cuddly just like a teddy bear, I love my Darcey princess. Do you like it?"

Laughing under his breath, Matthew replies, "That's beautiful. Your name's Darcey, what a pretty name."

"Thanks. My big sister Leah got my name for me."

"Oh, and how many sisters do you have, Darcey?"

"I have two sisters my Leah and my Hana. I also have a brother, his name is Simon."

"Wow, that's very cool."

"Yeah, I like them sometimes."

Laughing again, Matthew responds, "Just sometimes?"

"We all don't have the same daddy and they don't like my daddy too."

"Oh, okay."

Unaware of what to say next, they both sit in silence. Darcey begins swinging her little legs as they dangle from the bench.

"What's your name?"

"My name's Matthew."

"Who's this pretty lady in the picture?"

"Well, little Darcey, that's actually my little girl. Her name is Evelyn Jade and she's gone missing."

Darcey gasps and says, "So you lost her?"

"Yes, I lost her and that's why it's very important that you always stay close with your mummy and daddy."

"My teacher always says *stranger danger*."

"Yes, Darcey. Like *stranger danger*."

"You're a stranger."

Smirking, Matthew replies, "Yes, I am, you're very right. But, I'm okay. I'm not going to take you, darling."

"Your little girl was taken?"

"Yes, she was taken from me."

"Aw, that's so sad." A small tear forms in Darcey's eye as she looks to the picture on the leaflet. Looking back up to Matthew she says, "It's going to be okay. You will find her. I will help you."

Finished with her call, Darcey's mum storms over to the bench. "Sorry, is she bothering you? Darcey, come on."

"No, not at all."

Taking a proper look at Matthew and instantly judging him, Darcey's mum looks as if she's wondering whether he's some sort of molesting paedophile. Grabbing her little girl's hand, she begins pulling Darcey away. Desperately trying to show her mummy the leaflet, Darcey says, "Look, Mummy, the man lost his daughter. I'm going to help him find her."

"Yep, sure you are, darling. Come on, give the, erm, man his leaflet back." Once again pulling on her arm, the impatient mother struggles to drag her daughter away. Resisting her mother's strength, Darcey says, "No, Mummy, we can help him."

Clearly annoyed at her daughter's rebellious behaviour, she responds harshly, "I – said – let's – go – Darcey."

She rips the leaflet from Darcey's hand and throws it back on the bench. Darcey begins to cry as they walk away. Feeling angry but unable to do anything about it, Matthew turns away before he lashes out and gives this woman a few home truths about her parenting abilities, or lack thereof. Matthew lights another cigarette and in frustration grabs the stack of leaflets. Furious, he stands and aggressively pushes his way through the busy pathways, not caring whether he hurts or offends passers-by. And, thanks to his current homeless, neglected look, no one is brave enough to stand up to him. They simply snarl at Matthew for his rude and impolite ways, muttering under their breath. As he pushes his way through one group, Matthew thumps one well-dressed individual in the back. Wearing a shark grey suit with a white shirt and quirky emerald green bow tie, the man had been standing outside smoking and enjoying the company of his friends. After the initial shock of being hit by a stranger, he looks at Matthew in disgust. In an eccentric posh accent he says, "Pftt. You know the saying, 'beware the unloved'? Well, this is why. Rude behaviour."

Gritting his teeth and choosing to ignore the insult, Matthew's fully aware that he could simply snap this young boy into two pieces if he truly desired. But, instead, he clenches his fists and decides to keep walking. He puffs on his cigarette until it has disappeared, and as the nicotine surges around his body he feels a tiny bit calmer. Matthew leans against a tree outside one of the pubs near the car park and closes his eyes. A few minutes pass and he somehow manages to regain his composure and gather his thoughts. Shaking his head, he looks at the leaflets in his hand. Seeing his Evelyn Jade, his mouth turns up into a smile. But the smile doesn't reach his sorrowful eyes.

Feeling his heart breaking into thousands of pieces, Matthew reminds himself why he's doing this. His purpose is greater than the ignorance of others. Almost instantly, his strength returns. He has come so far. There is absolutely no way he's giving up. The one thing he will never do in his life is give up on his daughter. Throwing the cigarette butt on the ground, Matthew returns to the current task in hand, once again attempting to reach out to the public. Sadly, once again, not a single person is giving him the time of day. Matthew doesn't care that he's being ignored. He has a burning desire to get Eve back. Little Darcey has sparked the parental love inside of him. Oblivious to the finer details of his surroundings, Matthew fails to notice something important. Standing in the distance overseeing every single one of his movements are DCS Terry and DC Flores.

Holding a coffee in his hand, DCS Terry looks to his colleague and says, "So, when it comes to judgement day, do we believe he has done this?"

DC Flores replies, "For someone who has apparently committed murder, he's either really mentally unwell and has convinced himself that she's still alive, or, she really is alive. What I will say is I can't call it just yet, but you can't blame the guy for trying if she is still alive. He has barely stopped to rest. Even I'm tired and I'm just watching. Would you really be able to convince yourself to that extreme if you genuinely knew that the person was dead?"

"You see, that's what we have to try and do. The mind of a psychopath, murderer and someone with severe mental health issues, if unmedicated, can truly have these sorts of disturbing effects. He could pass a polygraph test right now based on his beliefs."

"Yes, but surely that—"

"No, just because someone believes they're innocent doesn't mean they are. It would help our case if we had a body."

"Yes, but that's the thing – if she has been taken, there wouldn't be one."

DCS Terry is unconvinced. "So you believe one man can be that unlucky? His wife gets murdered tragically and then sometime down the line he loses his only child as well and no one can find her body?"

"I'm not saying that's what I believe right now, but what I am saying is I wouldn't rule it out."

"Well, to be continued, DC Flores. He's on the move again." Walking towards the bin nearby, he throws his takeaway coffee cup away and says, "Come on, cheeky, let's go."

Smirking and shaking her head slightly at her superior's choice of words, DC Flores follows him back to their vehicle. As soon as they sit inside, DCS Terry's phone begins ringing, "It's the gaffa." Answering the call, he says, "Terry speaking."

"You got an update for me, Tez?" says Chief Inspector Lamont.

"Not really, subject is just returning to his vehicle now so we're just about to follow. Flores is driving."

"Don't you lose that bastard. I think he's going to lead you right to where he has buried her. Where are you now?"

"Oh, don't worry, we haven't taken our sights off him. We're in Chester town centre. He just keeps trailing up north."

"Up north?"

"Yeah, we just keep going up. Probably going to end up in the highlands at this rate."

"Yeah, I bet that's where the sick fucker has hidden her body."

"Wouldn't surprise me."

There is the muffled sound of someone else speaking in the background and Lamont says, "Yeah, sure, tell them I'm on my way now."

"Huh?" DCS Terry replies, confused.

"Right, got to go," Lamont says sharply. "I want updates emailed to all involved in *Operation Bee Sting* on a regular basis. Get DC Flores to sort it, that's what she's there for. Women are better at that paperwork crap, that's why I sent her with you."

Laughing, DCS Terry replies, "Subtle as always, Monty. Don't worry, we'll sort it out."

As he ends the call, chuckling to himself, DC Flores gives her mischievous colleague a look.

"What's so funny?"

"Nothing, you know what he's like. As subtle as a brick to the face."

"Why, what's he said?"

Avoiding the truth, as he doesn't want to put DC Flores in a mood due to being stuck with her twenty-four seven, DCS Terry simply says, "Nothing, he just wants us to send more of a paperwork trail."

"Oh, now I get it. Knowing the sexist pig that he is, he's made a comment about the woman doing the paperwork graft?"

Laughing at how quickly she has clicked on to this, DCS Terry says, "Hey, you heard my reply, I said we'll sort it out, so don't look at me." As Matthew's vehicle pulls out of the car park, thankful for the distraction DCS Terry continues, "He's pulling out. Follow him."

CHAPTER EIGHTEEN

What's the Big Secret...?

Lewis is exhausted, even though he has slept right through the morning and it's now midday. Desperate to rehydrate himself, he goes downstairs to get a drink from the kitchen to cure his dry throat. Jesse and Eve are there, having a heated, but quiet, discussion next to the cooker. Too tired to care what their conversation is about and not wanting to get involved, Lewis decides it's best to leave it alone. Scratching his head and yawning, he enters the front room. Throwing himself on the sofa, he grabs the remote control and switches on the television. Although he can't remember the events that took place in his horrific nightmare last night, he can however recall that he woke up sporadically throughout most of the night. As he flicks to the news, his phone begins to ring. He sees Ben's name flashing on the screen and answers straight away.

"Safe, bro, where you at?" Lewis says, his over-the-top Mancunian accent coming through.

"At home, bro." Ben replies with his Irish twang. "We going to that MC night tonight? Sounds sick."

"Yeah, bro, I'll check it with Eve. Me mum's in hospital at the minute, though, with our Hope. Might need to see if it's okay to leave her boyfriend with the kids."

"Sweet, I'll check in with the lads. What time do you wanna head out?"

Just as Lewis is about to reply, Eve and Jesse appear at the door. Eve walks into the front room while Jesse makes his way past the doorway and heads straight upstairs. Smiling at her, Lewis says to Ben, "Just one sec, bro, Eve's just walked in the room. I'll ask her now."

"Sound."

Looking confused, Eve says, "Ask me what?"

"Babe, the lads wanna head up to a big MC night in town tonight. You fancy it?"

"Yes, that sounds cool. Is…" Eve trails off, her face turning a pasty shade. Her lips look grey. Grabbing her stomach, she runs out of the room and heads straight upstairs to the bathroom.

Slightly concerned, and unsure what just happened and why, Lewis says to Ben, "Safe, bro, I'm gonna head out. Shout me later, yeah?"

"Safe, I'll check with the lads. Hit you up later, yeah?"

"Safe bro, laters."

Putting the phone down, Lewis makes his way up the stairs after Eve. The bathroom door is closed and he can hear violent retching sounds. Tapping on the door, he shouts, "Eve, baby, you okay?"

There is no answer, only the sound of something sloshing into the toilet bowl.

"Eve, you okay?"

"Yeah," replies Eve weakly, her voice hoarse.

The sloshing sounds resume with a vengeance.

Lewis attempts to open the bathroom door but soon realises it is locked from the inside. Feeling helpless and extremely anxious, he goes to look for Eve's dad. He makes his way into his mum's bedroom, expecting to see Jesse there, but is surprised to discover that the room is empty and the bed is perfectly made. He heads to Freddie's room, assuming that maybe Jesse is tending to him. Peering his head in, Lewis sees that Freddie's room is also empty and his bed is perfectly made. Now *really* confused, as he was sure he had just seen Jesse heading upstairs, Lewis makes his way to Terence and Rupert's room. Their room is also empty. And, much like the continuing theme throughout, their beds are also immaculately made up. Returning to the bathroom, he can still hear Eve throwing up inside.

"Babe, I'm trying to find your dad for you. Just bear with me." He places his head against the door, feeling powerless. "Are you okay?" he asks gently.

Still no answer. Growing increasingly concerned, Lewis decides once again to go on the hunt for Jesse, except this time he makes his way downstairs. Not only is he unable to find Jesse, his brothers are also nowhere to be seen. Standing in the front room in a panic, Lewis grabs his mobile, and, just as he's searching for his nana Dorothy's number, he feels an intense chill coming from behind him. Stopping what he was doing and freezing, Lewis slowly turns his head and peers over his shoulder. He jumps slightly at the sight of a very grey and pale-looking Eve. She's staring at him through the gap in her hair which hangs on either side of her face. With dark rings around her eyes, she looks as if she has handed her soul to the afterlife. Scared, Lewis says, "Eve, you made me jump. Is everything okay?"

Eve quietly croaks, "Yes."

Guiding her towards the sofa, Lewis replies, "You look terrible." He instantly realises the insult he's just given Eve, and stutters as he attempts to rectify this and remove himself from the hole he has just potentially dug. "I mean, erm... what I actually meant was... erm... You look poorly, baby." Desperate to redeem himself, he guides Eve towards the sofa and, as he lays her down, he tucks her up with a blanket. Kneeling next to Eve and stroking her hair away from her face, he whispers, "Baby, I'm trying to find your dad, but he ain't about and neither are the boys."

"They're gone," Eve says.

"Gone? What do you mean? Gone where?"

"To the hospital."

"Oh, right. Had me worried then."

"Why?"

Hesitating slightly, Lewis replies, "Nar, nothing, just the way you said they're gone."

Rolling her eyes, Eve responds with, "What do you mean by that?" She pauses, but not long enough for Lewis to respond before she says, "Do you really think my dad's just going to steal your brothers in broad daylight and leave me behind? Seriously, Lewis? Don't be so paranoid."

"Nar, I didn't mean it like… erm…" Once again finding himself at a loss for words, Lewis scratches his head. He knows he's offended Eve and doesn't want to continue to do the same, so he says, "Baby, just ignore me. Can I get you a drink or anything?"

"No, I'm fine."

"Okay, I'll ring Ben now and tell him to leave the gig tonight."

"Don't do that. It's fine, we'll go. It will be good to see everyone and get out the house for a bit. I'll be okay, I think I just ate something dodgy."

"Are you sure? I don't mind staying in." Cuddling up to Eve, he cheekily says, "We could play doctors and patients and I could look after you?"

Smirking, Eve says, "As tempting as that sounds, I want to get away from the little ones for a bit. Honestly, let's go – I could do with laugh."

"Okay, but only if you're sure. I think I had a leaflet somewhere. Let me grab it and we'll check out who's playing." Getting up off the sofa, Lewis makes his way into the dining room. Straight away he shouts, "WHAT THE FUCK?!" and runs back into the front room. In a fluster he says, "Eve, where's all my mum's pictures gone from off the wall?" Not getting a quick enough answer from Eve, he panics, saying, "Seriously, she's gonna go mental."

"For fuck's sake, chill out, Lewis. And stop shouting – it's hurting my ears. My dad has taken them to get cleaned."

Unlike most people who wouldn't believe a single word of this, Lewis, a sixteen-year-old boy, hasn't the first idea about cleaning picture frames. Innocent and naïve, he doesn't bother to question Eve any further. He's just relieved they've not been broken. "Oh right, phew," he says. Then, trying to justify his panic: "That's mum's shrine to dad. It would destroy her if that went missing." Making his way back across to Eve, he says, "I'm sorry, baby. Just ignore me."

"It's okay."

Lying next to her, he brings his legs up and moulds himself around her body. Getting cosy, they snuggle into one another. Holding Eve tightly in his arms, with his chin resting on her head, he smells her hair, taking in the moment with his girl. As the pair are enjoying the peace and quiet, Lewis's phone suddenly rings. This time it's Renato. Answering the call, Lewis says, "Yo, safe bro."

"Ben just rang about this MC night tonight. You in?"

Looking to Eve and kissing her on the head, Lewis says, "Not sure yet, bro, Eve's not too well."

"Don't listen to him, Renz," Eve shouts. "We're coming. I'll be fine."

"That's my girl!" Renato yells louds enough for Eve to hear. "See you later."

"See you later, Renz," Eve hollers.

"Lewis, everyone who's anyone is going to be there tonight. You know that, don't you? You gotta come," Renato says.

"I know, yeah. Don't worry, we'll be there."

"What time you goin' town?"

"Was thinking about half seven."

"Sweet, see you then." Renato raises his voice again to say, "See you later, Eve, hope you're feeling better."

"Thanks, Renz. I'll see you later."

As Lewis ends the call, suddenly a distressed expression crosses his face. An instant shooting pain travels through his brain. Suddenly, uninvited, a flashback from the nightmare he endured last night surfaces at the forefront of his mind. Shaking the image out of his head, Lewis shouts, "Fuck!"

With a concerned look upon her face, Eve glances to Lewis and says, "What's wrong?"

"Nothing, just a pain in my head."

"You sure?"

Looking to Eve, Lewis replies, "Yeah, baby, it's nothing."

Putting out his arms, Lewis cuddles into her.

Stroking his head, Eve says, "I feel like you have something on your mind, Lew."

The words are on the tip of his tongue, but Lewis doesn't want Eve to think he's some sort of wimp or psycho by telling her the strange goings on inside his head at the minute. And yet, he feels as though he needs to share what's happening with someone, and Eve being the only one around, he bites the bullet. "Okay, so I have a question."

"Go on, then, what is it?"

"So… You won't judge me, baby?"

"I won't, you can trust me. Spit it out."

"Have you ever had like, a nightmare that's felt proper real? Like it's true life happening rather than in your head?" Getting slightly frustrated as he knows it sound ridiculous, he says, "Ah, it's hard to explain, you know what I mean. It's like you're proper living in a real-life horror story." He pauses but without giving Eve time to respond, he continues, "Right, like – you know, like the horror movies, innit? Well, they always have it where some psycho is chasing after you, yeah, but it feels proper real. You know what I mean?"

Eve remains silent for a while, her head resting on his. Finally she says, "In answer to your question, yes I have."

Lewis is shocked. He was expecting her to call him crazy. "Really?!"

"Yes."

Becoming intrigued, Lewis lifts his head and shuffles round so that he's facing her. Happy that someone else has experienced this, he continues to quiz her. "So, erm, what do you think it means? Like, does it even mean anything? You know what I mean – is it like depending on what you dream about and who, or not?"

In a gentle and confident tone, she replies, "You embrace it."

"Huh?"

"Exactly what I just said. You embrace it. When I embraced my beautiful nightmare, I became free to be the real me. The fate that had been aligned for my path – I now get to live it every day. I get to live my purpose because I embrace all that I am, including my beautiful nightmares."

"What do you mean 'embrace it'?"

"Okay, so next time you have one, submit yourself." Lewis stares at her, still confused. Eve clarifies: "When it happens again, just say the words 'I surrender my soul'. Then what will happen is all reality just goes away and you'll feel amazing. Try it. What have you got to lose? It's just a dream."

Curious and apprehensive, but swayed by Eve's confidence, Lewis says, "Alright, sweet then, next time I'll say that."

"Right, come here now, I need a cuddle."

As Lewis places his head back onto Eve's chest, she smiles deceitfully. Her eyes light up with an air of secrecy.

CHAPTER NINETEEN

Secrets to the Grave

I t's just past two in the afternoon and Wythenshawe Hospital is crowded. In ward seven, where Alice and baby Hope are staying, the phones are ringing off the hook and people are rushing around everywhere. Medical staff are walking briskly up and down the corridor or standing at patients' bedsides reviewing observation charts and test results, all of them trying to do their jobs to the best of their ability in this busy environment.

It's the height of visiting hour and that means one thing: utter bedlam. The continual wave of overly concerned relatives is one of the worst parts about working in any hospital. Assuming their loved one is the only person who requires actual care, visitors are, for the most part, more trouble to have on the ward than the patients themselves. They constantly create issues and incessantly moan.

All staff, whether support staff, nurses or doctors, are in the firing line. Anyone wearing a hospital uniform is in line for an earful.

"Excuse me – excuse me."

"Yes."

"Well, erm, my mother has been left all day without having her bed changed or even asked if she wants food and water."

"I don't think that's actually true now is it."

"How fucking dare you? Are you saying my mother's a liar?"

"Can I just refer you to the sign." The member of the hospital team points to the sign above her head which reads, "**Abusive behaviour against any member of staff will not be tolerated and will result in you being asked to leave**".

Relenting slightly, the angry daughter says, "Fine, sorry for my language, but can you blame me when my mother's telling me she's dying in there because of your lack of care."

"Your mother's Mrs Blinky, yes?"

"That's correct."

"So that would make you Dawn?"

"Yes."

"Dawn – your mother has been showing signs of dementia. I can assure you she has been well cared for all day by myself and my staff members. I can show you the sheets if you like, everything is logged."

"Dementia. How, erm, what, erm, I…" Dawn walks away from the desk muttering, "I need to be with my mother right now."

Yet more fretful relatives arrive, rushing to get to their poorly family member's designated bedside. Their hands are filled with a variety of different coloured balloons, treats, flowers, cosy pyjamas and other nice gifts, which they balance awkwardly while attempting to watch where they're walking.

"Georgie can you move, please."

"Mummy, where's Aunty Valarie?"

"That way, Georgie. Will you just watch where you're going? Follow your brother."

Ward seven is one of the busiest wards in the hospital. Each of the rooms and communal hospital bays are now at maximum capacity. Adults stand like giants and hover around the bedsides, while mischievous youngsters who are not being watched conspire with one another and swing around the place, pressing buttons they shouldn't be and generally making nuisances of themselves. The atmosphere is chaotic.

Thankfully, having been listed as a high-risk priority, Alice and baby Hope are safe from the fast-paced fuss taking place on the ward. They have been assigned to a private room. Room seven isn't particularly big, but it's cosy and even has an en-suite bathroom. Alice is being shielded for good reason. She remains in a critical state and is not doing well. Feeble, drained, and having temporarily lost the use of her legs, Alice is confined to her hospital bed. Whatever is attacking her internal system is leaving her too weak to function. Her brain has gone into protection mode and is shutting down the movements of her physical body in a desperate bid to save her internal organs from any potential lasting damage. This mental shut down has restricted Alice dramatically.

Alice is attached to multiple monitors, which bleep continuously as they calculate her vital signs. Her heartrate and pulse are stable but slow. Her temperature and blood pressure, however, are quite the opposite. They're unexplainably rocketing, and then dramatically depleting, which in turn is causing Alice to become extremely delirious.

During the night, Alice inexplicably took a turn for the worse. The doctors managed to revive her and are keeping her stable by pumping drugs of all kinds into her system, but without a diagnosis or any idea as to why this has happened, each doctor and consultant that has assessed Alice has been left scratching their head with confusion. Greatly concerned about their patient's health, they have conducted test after test but still have no explanation for Alice's potentially life-threatening condition. They are keeping her alive and as pain free as possible, but they're nervous about the possibility of Alice dying in their care. For that reason, Alice has been placed on thirty-minute observational checks.

Not only do the nurses and doctors have to facilitate Alice's needs, they also have a new challenge to contend with as baby Hope is refusing to settle. The poorly little girl is crying relentlessly and has been for the past six hours.

In an effort to work out what is causing Alice's condition, the consultants have sent blood and urine samples and mouth swabs to the lab for testing. And from what little information has been fed back up to the ward from the technicians, it's clear to see that something isn't at all right, but no one has a clue what it is, so finding a cure is proving impossible.

Downstairs in the laboratories in the basement of the hospital, a sign saying "**Private and Confidential** – *Testing in Progress*" has been placed upon one of the white doors. Inside, the room is extremely bright. Machines of all kinds are everywhere and are analysing various pots and samples with white labels on them. Standing in their white coats and wearing blue latex gloves, are Zander, Jack and Emily. These three, highly qualified, medical scientists have been assigned the challenge of working out what is attacking Alice and Hope's bodies.

Zander and Emily are peering through their microscopes. Zander has Alice's blood specimen and Emily has Hope's. Standing by the interior window, Jack is preparing to examine Alice's DNA, slowly wiping the contents of her mouth swab onto the testing glass.

"Jack, can you come here please and check this out?" says Zander, sounding concerned.

Casually making his way to Zander, Jack says, "Sure."

After peering through the high resolution microscope, Jack looks up at Zander with a confused expression upon his face. Wiping his eyes to ensure he's not seeing things, Jack puts his eye back to the lens. It's clear to see that these highly trained scientists are both witnessing the same thing. Something illogical is happening. The unidentified element in Alice's body is attacking her blood cells. And, almost instantly, her cells are becoming weak. As Jack watches, the unknown substance is capturing Alice's DNA. No sooner has contact been made, her cells surrender as they shrivel and die. Baffled as this defies the certainties of science, Jack looks to Zander and says, "What the…"

"I know, right, what is that?"

"I've never seen anything like this." Gazing back into the microscope and fiddling with the focus, Jack continues, "They're just dying."

Standing at her workstation, Emily pulls back from her lens. "You guys, erm, you might want to take a look at this."

Zander makes his way across and takes a look. Without needing to focus the lens, he instantly gasps and steps back, "What on earth is that? Jack, you have to take a look into this one."

Already scratching his head and highly concerned, Jack makes his way across to Hope's blood specimen. This time, he too doesn't need to fiddle with the focus, he sees something is wrong. Unlike in Alice's sample, here the unidentified element is wrapping itself around Hope's DNA and multiplying at a rapid rate, becoming stronger and fiercer by the millisecond. Not only this, the substance is changing tone.

Looking to both Zander and Jack, Emily says, "What are we going to do? This can't be real, right? This is like some supernatural voodoo stuff. It's not real science, right? We're just seeing things."

Attempting to process what he's witnessing, looking more perplexed with every tick and tock of the clock, Jack says, "We need to get the higher ranks in to have a look at this. This is beyond anything I've ever seen."

Jack makes his way to the phone, but just as he pick it up, the room goes dark. A horrific screech penetrates their eardrums and an unknown force throws each of them across the room. Landing on the ground, Zander, Jack and Emily curl up into balls. They all cry out in pain at the noise circulating inside their minds. The energy within the room has changed. Unaided, the door locks. A vibrational shift takes place. There is a sudden loud crash as the glass from the interior windows and the machines smashes, hitting Zander, Jack and Emily.

Terrified, Emily screams. A huge shard of glass travels toward her at rapid speed and lands at the back of her throat. Instantly, the sharp shard slices through her carotid artery. Her neck pulsates and blood gushes from her mouth and travels down her chin. Her eyes wide open, Emily lies on the floor choking to her death.

Both Zander and Jack are completely unaware of Emily's critical state. It's too dark inside the room. Zander can hear the gasps of someone trying to take in oxygen. Frightened and not wanting to draw attention to his whereabouts in the room, Zander whispers shakily, "Jack, Emily?"

No sooner have the words left his mouth, one of the lights begins to flicker. Appearing from nowhere is a horrific vision of a teenage girl. Her jet-black hair is draped on either side of her face and her skin is grey and cracked. A sinister black liquid oozes from the cracks in her skin as she stares at Zander and Jack through the flickering light with her jet-black eyes. She slowly makes her way towards the crippled professionals on the floor. Everywhere she steps she leaves a smear of the thick black substance.

Struggling to breathe, Jack drags himself across the floor to where Zander sits. Reaching out to help his friend, Zander grabs Jack's arm and pulls him closer. Looking across to the shadowy girl, Zander shouts, "What do you want?"

No response. The dark figure stares at the two frightened individuals.

"Zander, oh my God, it's going to kill us." Crying, Jack tucks himself into Zander's arm, "I don't want to die."

In excruciating pain, Zander feels as if every bone in his body has been broken. Not giving up, Zander bravely speaks once more, "Please don't hurt us. Look, what do you want? Maybe we can help you."

She takes one step closer to Jack and Zander. As she opens her mouth to speak, the black substance gushes down her chin. "The time will arrive, soon you will see, this world was never yours to keep."

She raises her head slightly and twitches it to one side. Almost instantly, Zander and Jack hold their hands around their throats. Their airways are being restricted.

"*Temimi!*" she shouts.

She twitches her head once more and a scalpel flies across the room at great force, cutting Jack and embedding deep into his eye. Another head twitch and a filing cabinet speeds across the room towards Zander. The heavy metal structure hits him in the head and crushes his skull.

All three of them now lie lifeless.

Content, the shadowy girl makes her way across the room and uses the black substance to smear across the wall the word "MUORI". Taking the DNA samples, she disappears.

She has completed her task. Their secret has been taken to the grave.

Visiting time is still in full swing when Dorothy arrives at her daughter's private hospital room. She is keen to assist with the care of Alice and baby Hope. Due to the current high demand and shortness of staff, the nurses reluctantly, and temporarily, hand baby Hope over to Dorothy. This familiar face just might help to calm her. She is doing everything in her power in an attempt to care for baby Hope, but Dorothy is also not having much luck. Nothing is soothing this baby girl. Whatever it is that's upsetting Hope, it is leaving her inconsolable. It has gotten so bad, she won't accept cuddles, take her bottle or even keep her dummy in her mouth, which is normally the secret weapon.

Resembling a medicated zombie, Alice is lying completely still. The only part of her which is moving are her eyes. Gently blinking, every now and then, she glances across to her mum.

Singing a sweet melody, nannie Dorothy is desperately trying to make her precious granddaughter feel better, walking up and down the room in a rhythmic fashion. Dorothy is pulling out all her nannie special talents to help calm baby Hope but still, nothing is working. With no response, and at a loss as to what to do next, Dorothy looks to Alice and says, "I think we should call for the doctor. Nothing's working, my dear."

As her granddaughter's screams get louder and Alice remains unresponsive, Dorothy ventures across the room and takes a closer look at her daughter. The reality of Alice's current physical state is devastating. This isn't the image Dorothy was expecting. Just yesterday, Alice was full of life and wearing her usual radiant smile. Well, she isn't anymore. Trying to fight back the tears at the sight of her daughter's rapid deterioration, Dorothy's struggling to hold it together. It's breaking her heart to see her precious one and only daughter looking so lifeless. Kneeling at the side of Alice's bed, Dorothy says, "Alice, my dear, can you hear me?"

Alice is staring out the window. Her eyes gradually turn towards her mum. Her expression blank, Alice blinks and still, she says nothing. Filling up with tears once more, Dorothy is in denial and doesn't want to process this image. Her Alice, her baby girl, her princess, her bright smiling precious daughter is no longer there. Feeling an element of rejection, and not wishing to accept her daughter's state as it's too painful, Dorothy holds Alice's hand and says, "Let us pray."

Closing her eyes, almost instantly Dorothy sees an image of Alice when she was a young girl, wearing a dark green and black chequered dress with a black collar and puffy short sleeves. Along with this traditional nineteen eighties little girl look, Alice's hair is resting neatly upon her shoulders. In this snapshot image, young Alice has just turned six years of age and is in her bedroom playing. Fiddling with her brand-new doll set on the floor, she's happily singing away to herself. Little Alice is embracing her imagination and remains oblivious to the fact that her mum is standing in the doorway watching her play.

In this vision, Dorothy rests her head on the doorframe and stares at her daughter with sheer admiration, love and feeling nothing but strength. Smiling at young Alice's innocence, and overwhelmed with relief, she wipes the single tear from her cheek. This tear which has fallen from her blackened eye. This memory is of the special kind. It's a memory she will never forget. This day was the day she allowed courage to take over. On this day she left her abusive husband, Alice's father, and became free. Her first day as a single mother and not a punching bag. And, my goodness, was she happy about it.

Back in the hospital room, with her eyes still closed, as the memory fades Dorothy hears the screams of baby Hope in her arms. Opening her eyes, she looks to Alice and sees that not so much as a flicker has taken place. Looking to her granddaughter, who is screaming at the top of her voice, Dorothy notices there are no tears falling from her eyes. Aware that she is powerless to help, she makes her way across the room and wraps baby Hope inside multiple blankets using what she calls the sausage roll technique. Dorothy then places Hope inside the hospital cot. She's under no illusion. She knows there's nothing she can do to help Hope. And right now, all she truly desires to do is hold Alice.

Leaving Hope to cry, she makes her way back to her daughter. Perching herself on the edge of the bed, Dorothy leans across and kisses her on the forehead. Alice is like an oven. Stroking her hair back from off her face, Dorothy tucks it behind Alice's ear in the hope of cooling her down. Shuffling up and lying on the bed next to Alice, she reaches over and hugs her daughter tightly. Breathing her in, Dorothy whispers, "Lord only knows how much I love you, Alice. Lord only knows how much I need you. Lord only knows I would die for you. Please, my dear, come back to us, we cannot lose you."

Holding her, Dorothy suddenly experiences a flashback from last night. Embodied with guilt after reading Alice's personal and private letter, Dorothy feels she has betrayed her daughter and wants to confess. Pulling back slightly, an expression of shame darkens her face. Looking to Alice, she says, "My dear, I have to tell you something."

Saying nothing, Alice continues to stare blankly her mum's way.

Unable to make eye contact, Dorothy tucks Alice's head under her chin. Stroking her daughter's hair once more, nervous, Dorothy bites the bullet and says, "I'm so sorry. I don't know how to say this, my dear." Trying to block out Hope's screams so she can tell her daughter her sin, Dorothy closes her eyes and continues, "I read your letter from Phil. I'm sorry. I know I shouldn't have. I was so worried and just wanted to know..."

But before she can finish her sentence, the door bursts open. Running into the room with their little legs flapping at high speed, full of life and waving drawings they have made, are Terence and Rupert. And not too far behind them is Freddie. He too has his hands full. Freddie is carrying a huge bouquet of deep red roses, organised with perfection and sitting inside a beautifully designed box, with cream lace wrapped around it and a huge ruby red silk bow on the front. Trapped inside her medicated state, not so much as a flinch comes from Alice.

Wiping her eyes to conceal the tears, not wanting the boys to see her pain, Dorothy gets up off the edge of the bed. Turning around with a huge over the top smile, she shouts, "Boys!"

Racing and almost pushing one another over, both Terence and Rupert jump on the bed. Battling, these two mini boys cannot wait to hug and kiss their nannie and mummy.

Alice stares at her boys as they both bounce on her hospital bed with excitement. A single tear rolls down her motionless face.

Dorothy watches as Freddie slowly trails into the room with the bouquet in front of his face. He walks straight over to Hope who is still in her hospital cot. He looks shocked by her current screaming state. Placing the heavy bouquet onto the side, he makes his way back over to his little sister. Peering in, he sees she's spat her dummy out. Unaware of the severity of his mum's and Hope's medical condition, he seems to think her dummy will solve the problem. He attempts to place it inside her mouth to try and stop her from crying. He becomes annoyed himself as she resists. Seeming grumpy and slightly tired, Freddie looks to his nannie Dorothy and says, "Wow, what's her problem?"

"Oh, nothing to worry about, my love, she's just a little under the weather." Making her way across to Freddie, Dorothy puts out her arms, "Come here you and give your nannie a hug."

Grabbing Freddie and squeezing him tightly, Dorothy tries her hardest to refrain from crying. Closing her eyes, she's gathering the strength to let him go and keep a brave expression on her face. As her eyes gently flicker open, suddenly, something catches her sight. Peering up at the doorway, she sees Jesse entering. The moment Jesse's foot lands inside the room, Hope's scream hits its highest peak. Like a supersonic sound, her scream is loud enough to pierce eardrums. Squeezing their eyelids tightly together, each of the boys, along with Dorothy, place their hands over their ears, desperately trying to block out the deafening sound. Freddie shouts, "Ouch! Someone get her to stop."

Terence and Rupert both jump under the covers of Alice's bed. Little Rupert instantly begins crying. Burying his head in the blanket, Terence shouts at the top of his voice, "Stop, Hope, please stop crying."

Each one of them has reacted to the sound. Well, all, that is, except Jesse. Placing the overnight bag he's carrying on the floor, he closes the door behind him. In no rush, and without making eye contact with anyone, Jesse heads straight across to Hope.

Reaching inside the cot, he places his hands around Hope's body. Securing his grip, he picks her up. As soon as Jesse makes direct physical contact with Hope, she stops not only screaming, but crying too. This tiny inconsolable baby girl is now silent and content. Shocked, Dorothy cannot believe what she's just witnessed. Her jaw drops; she is literally lost for words. Uncovering his ears, Freddie says, "Thank goodness for that."

Jesse cradles Hope with a smug grin on his face. Finally looking across the room and engaging in direct eye contact with Dorothy, he doesn't say a single word. He doesn't need to. Not wanting to create a scene, Dorothy chooses not to react or acknowledge what has just happened. Although her facial expression says it all. Scowling at Jesse, she says, "Where are Lewis and Eve?"

"Oh, hi to you, too, Dorothy, how nice of you to acknowledge me in the room—"

"Jesse, stop playing games," Dorothy interrupts. "I'd prefer if you answered the question and didn't try to goad me in front of my sick daughter and my grandchildren."

"Goad you?"

"Yes, goad me."

"Hmm, I'm not sure what you are referring to, Dorothy. I mean I've been looking after your grandchildren, and not only that, I've just managed to console this little one. Oh, sorry, did you?" His smug grin growing, Jesse continues with a sarcastic tone, "After all, Dorothy, let's face facts. I don't have the problem, you do. If you chose to think I'm 'goading you', as you say, then that's on you. I'm merely making a point that you don't usually acknowledge my existence."

"Okay, whatever you say, Jesse. I'm not getting into this pettiness with you. Are you going to answer the question or not?"

"Sure, Dorothy. As far as I'm aware, they're at home."

"Didn't Lewis want to come and see his mum?"

Rolling his eyes, Jesse replies, "Dorothy, he's sixteen. He wants to be with Eve. He doesn't want to be running around the hospital. He knows his mum is being looked after, so why worry him?"

"Worry him? His mum is in a potentially life-threatening state and you don't think he should be here?"

Picking up on what his nannie has just said, Freddie says, "What...? Mum's going to die?"

The realisation of what she has just blurted out sinks in for Dorothy. Wrapped in her own selfish emotions, she didn't think before she spoke. His back to Jesse, Freddie frantically looks to his nannie for an answer. Meanwhile, cradling Hope, Jesse smirks. Laughing under his breath, he quietly says, "Go on, Dorothy, get out of this one."

Regretting her words and trying to not cause any more psychological damage to her grandson, Dorothy says, "Erm, of course not, mate."

Crying, Freddie says, "So why did you just say that?"

"I'm sorry, Freddie, I didn't mean it, it was just an expression. It's not the truth." Kneeling down to Freddie's level, Dorothy continues, "Come here, my handsome boys. Nannie needs a hug from you all."

Gently climbing over their mum to reach his nannie, Terence is the first to jump on his nannie's knee, closely followed by Rupert. Dorothy snuggles up and receives their love.

"Please, Nannie, what's wrong with mum?" Freddie whispers in her ear.

"Don't worry, she's just tired," she replies. Masking the sadness, Dorothy begins chuckling and continues, "Wouldn't you be if you had to listen to your sister screaming all night?"

Smiling, Freddie replies, "Suppose so, yeah." Seeming content with the answer he's received, he asks, "Can I come stay at yours tonight?"

Dorothy would love nothing more than to have Freddie stay over but tonight she has other plans. Tonight she's on a mission. She has decided that she's going to spend the evening finding out as much information as she can about Jesse and Eve. "Oh, my dear, tonight I already have plans," she says, but seeing the sadness on Freddie's face and feeling terrible she continues, "What's the date today?" Checking her phone, she sees that it's Friday sixth July. "Okay, prince, shall I tell you what?"

"What?"

"Tomorrow I'm completely free. What do you say, do you want to stay tomorrow instead?"

Beaming with happiness, Freddie jumps up and down as he says, "Yes, just me though, right?"

Smiling, she replies, "Well, if no one else wishes to stay over, then yes, just you."

"I'll make sure they don't know where I'm staying. Ha!"

Overseeing the events, Jesse stands in the corner of the room with Hope still tightly grasped in his arms. Looking to Alice, he's satisfied and content with her current paralysed state. As he gazes down at baby Hope, his eyes hold an air of secrecy hidden deep inside of them. These two individuals are connected as one. Chiming loudly throughout the ward, a bell is ringing. That can only mean one thing: visiting time is now over.

CHAPTER TWENTY

The Call You've Been Waiting For

Leaning into the white porcelain sink, Matthew throws warm water onto his face. Using the paper towels provided, he pats his skin. His hands placed at either side of the sink, Matthew breathes heavily. As water continues to drip from his face, he looks at himself in the mirror, taking in the realities of his current state. Suddenly, he sees Jezebel in the reflection. A huge rage boils up inside of him and he punches the mirror, shouting, "Bitch!"

It creates a huge crack in the mirror, Matthew's blood is spattered across the glass. Looking to the mirror once more, he sees she's gone! Desperately trying to catch his breath as adrenaline surges around his body, Matthew notices that his knuckles are bleeding. Not wanting anyone to see, he rushes out of the pub and heads down the street.

Panicking, and aware that he needs to clean up, Matthew looks around and sees a shop about half a mile down the road. Thankfully, it's still open – he can vaguely see people entering and leaving. Constantly checking over his shoulder to ensure that he isn't being chased down the road, he heads toward the store. Once he has run far enough away to feel in the clear, Matthew slows down and makes his way inside the small family run shop. He rushes to the medication stand and grabs a bandage and some safety pins. Continuing to select items for his DIY first aid kit, Matthew gets a bottle of water, a bottle of vodka and then walks to the till.

"That's a weird combination," the friendly cashier says, attempting a joke. Winking he continues, "Ha! Aye, is the water so that you don't get a fuzzy head in the morning?" Matthew remains silent. Even though he has not received a response to his question, the jolly cashier continues, "I know what you're about, aye." Tapping his head he says, "Up there for thinking and down there for dancing. Ha! Very clever. Well, it looks like you're in for a good night."

Matthew is not amused one bit. He stares at the cashier blankly. Wanting to pay for his items and get out of the shop, eventually Matthew says, "Sure," in a desperate attempt to put an end to the conversation.

Obviously sensing the awkward energy, the cashier glances at the blood dripping from Matthew's hand and replies, "Erm, okay, so that's seventeen pounds eighty pence, please."

Matthew passes him the money. With the uncomfortable pleasantries over, Matthew grabs his purchased items and instantly leaves the shop. Marching at a fast pace, with his head down low, he makes his way towards the back street where his vehicle is parked. Unlocking the car door, Matthew throws the vodka and bandage on the front seat. Twisting the plastic cap and opening the bottle of water, he tips the contents over his knuckles. Cleaning the blood and tiny shards of glass from his hand, Matthew closes his eyes and breathes deeply as it sends shooting pains up his arm. In agony, he struggles to hold his screams inside. Wanting to numb the pain, Matthew opens the bottle of vodka and gulps the toxic liquid down. Scrunching his features as it warms his insides, Matthew impulsively pours a small amount of this sterile liquid over his wounds. Content with the clean-up, he then begins wrapping the bandage around his hand to conceal his injuries.

Tired and feeling sorry for himself, Matthew has decided he's not searching for his daughter this evening. The only desire he has right now is to get drunk and forget all about his depressing life for one evening.

With the darkness of the night fast approaching, the streetlamps begin to flicker on. Standing behind his car, Matthew searches in the boot for any items of clothing he can change into. Fishing out a crumpled shirt and a shark-grey blazer, Matthew puts these on. He doesn't find any trousers to change into but much to his surprise, he does find some smart looking black shoes pushed into the corner. Taking off the uncomfortable boots and slipping into the shoes, Matthew's relieved as the soft leather begins hugging his swollen feet. Matthew's present look isn't the tidiest but it's smart enough to produce a somewhat respectable appearance. Locking his car and straightening himself up, he makes his way across the road to Chester Racecourse.

Since his continued mission to find his daughter is proving to be unsuccessful, Matthew's convinced himself that this betting venue has a dual purpose. Not only can he get drunk to the point where he no longer knows his own name, he can, in his mind, also soak up some luck. Arriving at the front entrance, aware that he's slightly intoxicated, Matthew thinks fast and manages to charm his way through.

Inside, the place is a sea of glamour. All the beautiful ladies and handsome looking gents are dressed up to the nines, standing in groups laughing and enjoying each other's company. The energy within the room is buzzing. Bypassing the beautiful people, Matthew heads straight for the alcohol. Although it's crowded, he manages to push his way through the masses of bodies and perches himself at the bar. Looking at the multiple huge television screens scattered around up high, Matthew checks out this evening's runners. Straightaway, two horses catch his eye. Two chestnut-coloured five-furlong beauties with the odds stacked against them. Matthew's gambling sixth sense has kicked in. It's telling him that these runners are tonight's unexpected lucky big winners. He leaves the bar before ordering a drink. Making his way across to the betting desk, he grabs the wad of cash he has from his pocket and says, "I wanna place a monkey on Celerity and a monkey on Caledonian Gold."

Confused, the cashier says, "Monkeys?"

He has forgotten that he's no longer down south. This young girl doesn't understand his cockney slang. Laughing, he says, "Yeah, sorry sweet. I mean I wanna place a five-hundred-pound bet on each of those horses."

Embarrassed and laughing back, she says, "Don't worry, it's not a problem. I just didn't understand what a monkey was. I've not come across that one yet. Thanks for the heads up." Flirting slightly, she flutters her eyelashes as she continues, "So the horses are Celerity and Caledonian Gold?"

"Yeah."

"You sure you wanna do five hundred on each? I mean the odds aren't too clever on them two."

"Yeah, but think of the return." Smirking and feeling brave in his slightly intoxicated state, Matthew returns the flirty behaviour. "I'll tell you what, let's make this exciting. As you can see I'm a betting man. If both of those horses come in first place, I'll buy you a drink after work. What do you say..." Looking to her name badge he continues, "...Marilyn?"

"What, both come in first place?"

"Yeah, both of them, that's how confident I am."

"Okay, Mr Confident. If both horses come in first place, I'll be so impressed that I'll one hundred percent join you for a drink."

He puts out his hand and Marilyn shakes it. Collecting his ticket, Matthew says, "Deal. Celery and Callie, I already thank you." Kissing his ticket, he cheekily says, "See you later, Marilyn."

Smiling as she watches Matthew walk away she shouts, "We'll see."

Sat at the desk inside her home-based office, Dorothy is on the internet frantically searching for anything she can find relating to Jesse and Eve. But without their full names, she's struggling. Aware that Lewis and Eve are out this evening, she calls Lewis's mobile, hoping he will inadvertently relay the information she needs in his haste to get her off the phone. Lewis picks up. She can hear music blaring in the background.

"Nan, is everything okay?" Lewis shouts, sounding worried.

"Lewis, can you hear me?" Dorothy yells back. But unfortunately the noise is too loud.

"One sec, Nan, I can't hear you. Let me ring you back."

Hanging up, Dorothy waits in anticipation for Lewis to call her back. It feels as if an eternity has gone by when the phone eventually rings. Answering straightaway, Dorothy shouts, "Lewis, can you hear me?"

"Yeah, that's better, I can hear you now. What's up, is mum okay?"

"What, huh, yeah darling nothing to worry about. Where's Eve?"

"I've just left her with the group. I've come to the toilet where it's quieter to talk to you. Do you want me to go get her?"

Relieved, Dorothy says, "No, it's fine. Erm, Lewis, my dear, I'm trying to book train tickets for a special day out for us all, but they're asking for Eve's full name. As silly as it sounds, I don't actually know it, do you?"

"Erm, yeah, sure, it's Evelyn Honey." Someone shouts Lewis's name in the background. "Nan, look, I've gotta go back to the lads. Hope that helps."

"More than you'll ever know, my dear. Love you. Have a great night." Mission accomplished and much easier than anticipated.

"Thanks, Nan, love ya."

Ending the call, Dorothy instantly types Evelyn Honey into the search bar. She hits enter and waits for the results to come in...

On his way out of the toilet cubicle Lewis is met by Ben. Smiling, Ben says, "Come on, bro, you're gonna miss the best bit."

Scratching his head slightly, as though something doesn't feel right, Lewis puts his phone inside his trouser pocket and says, "Yeah, sorry bro, I'm coming now."

"Is everything okay, bro?"

"Yeah, I'm good. Just me Nan being random."

"Sweet, let's go."

Heading out of the toilets and through the crowd, the lads stagger back towards the group. They're all standing in a huddle in the same spot where Lewis left them, grinding in time with the beat of the music. Blending back in, Lewis and Ben shake their shoulders and smile at one another. They've each got a girl by their side. The usual suspects, Eve, Renato, Isaiah and Elijah, are there, and the group has joined ranks with some other friends. Also dancing in the circle are Laila, Alissa, Olivia, Izzy, Kaci and Joshua. They each have a drink in their hand and are enjoying the evening. The oversized bunch of excitable youths bounce up and down together, taking up a large section of the dance floor. Ben has found his way over to Kaci. Tall, curvy, beautiful and rebellious, Kaci has glasses perched on the bridge of her nose and long red hair. Kaci's parents have allowed her to bring a small bottle of vodka, which she has managed to sneak into the club inside her bag. She's slightly drunk, but she's having the time of her life with Ben.

Laila and Alissa are identical twins. They've joined ranks with the twin boys of the group, Isaiah and Elijah. These gorgeous dark-skinned girls are unique. Yes, they might look the same, but their personalities are far from similar. Dancing with Elijah, Alissa sips her cola, keeping her dancing with Elijah clean fun. Laila, on the other hand, is grinding all over Isaiah. She's drinking cola with vodka and she can't help but kiss the boy she likes, even though she knows if her dad finds out he will kill her. Tapping her sister on the shoulder, Alissa says, "Laila, dad will kill you if he finds out, stop it!"

Laughing, Laila replies, "Ha, well I might as well carry on, then, because it's only gonna be you who tells him."

"No, I won't," Alissa responds. Appearing annoyed, she shouts back, "Fine, do what you want, see if I care. He'll find out anyway when he picks us up and you're wasted."

"Yeah, but he won't know about Isaiah unless you tell him, which I know you will."

"I just said I won't."

"You promise?"

"I twin swear, I won't say anything to dad."

"Or mum?"

"Yes, or mum."

"Aw, thanks, sis."

Kaci dances her way over. Raising her voice so she can be heard over the music, she shouts, "You okay, girls?"

Smiling at her, Laila says, "We're all good, girl. Now let's see you shake that beautiful sassy booty of yours."

On the other side of the circle, Renato, Oliva, Joshua and Izzy are all dancing. They're drinking and enjoying the music. These four couldn't give a hoot right now about getting off with the opposite sex. Their favourite song has just hit the speakers and they're showcasing their best dirty grime moves.

Sweating and, grinding upon Lewis's body, Eve shouts in his ear, "Baby, I need to go outside, I feel a bit sick."

Lewis immediately looks at the lads and says, "Just taking Eve outside. She feels a bit sick, it's too hot in here."

Replying loud enough to be heard over the music, they all shout, "Sweet, bro."

"Stay here, yeah. Won't be long."

They make their way out of the jam-packed venue, Lewis holding Eve's hand as he gently pulls her towards the back doors. With an exit ahead, Eve lets go of Lewis's grip, and runs out of the building and heads to the back of a cabin. She goes out of sight of the party goers. Lewis is standing just behind her as she vomits. Concerned for his girl, Lewis holds Eve's hair back and says, "How much have you had to drink, baby?"

She throws up again. As soon as she stops, Eve spits one final time and says, "I haven't even been drinking. Are you that stupid, Lewis?"

"Huh, stupid?"

"Wow, you haven't worked it out yet, have you?"

"Worked what out... Baby, what's wrong?"

"Lewis, I'm pregnant!"

Lewis's eyes widen. Looking like he has just seen a ghost, Lewis is stiff.

"Lewis, did you hear what I said?"

Letting go of her hair, Lewis suddenly staggers backwards, he manages to lean on the wall for support. Eve makes her way to Lewis and guides him to the ground. She sits next to him. "I didn't want to tell you like this. My dad said I shouldn't tell you or your mum. Please don't say anything until we've worked this out."

Still in shock, Lewis says nothing. Suddenly they hear, "Lewis, Eve?" Olivia and Izzy have come outside to see if everything's okay with Eve. Making her way out from around the back of the cabin, Eve shouts, "Girls, won't be long, just having a moment with Lewis. We're all good, though."

Oliva shouts back, "You sure?"

"Yeah, lovely, we're fine."

Looking to Izzy, Olivia says, "Come on, let's leave them to it."

Both the girls head back inside to join the rest of the group. Turning around, Eve makes her way back to Lewis, who has his knees raised and his head firmly in his hands. As Eve sits next to him once more, he looks to her and says, "I'm going to be a dad?"

"Yeah, looks that way."

Surprisingly, Lewis reaches over, holds her in his arms and kisses her on the head as he whispers, "I promise I will support you both."

Matthew has been joined by Marilyn at the Chester Racecourse bar, which can only mean one thing... both Celerity and Caledonian Gold ranked and came in first place. Both in a drunken state, Matthew and Marilyn are blowing his substantial winnings on masses of alcohol. They've been joined by a huge group who are also scavenging drinks from his winnings. Matthew's huge financial gain has made him instantly popular with the bar patrons, and his ego is telling him to carry on and flash the cash and bask in the attention. Embracing his new-found popularity, Matthew's getting lost in the partying madness. He has completely forgotten about his true intention of finding his daughter. Making his way to the bar, Matthew shouts, "Another round on me!"

Shaking his head, the manager says, "I think you might have had enough, mate."

Furious at the suggestion and the rejection, Matthew shouts back, "What? Do you even know exactly what you're speaking to now, lad?"

"Huh?"

"Yeah, that's what I thought. You need to get back to work and make me and my people drinks for now."

"Sure mate, just wait there, I'll go and get someone to make your drinks for you."

"Yeah, see that's what I was talking about. Thank you, young man."

Looking Marilyn in the eye, Matthew wastes no time as he leans over and begins passionately kissing her. Accepting this, Marilyn runs her fingers through his hair and holds Matthew close. No sooner are the pair locked by passion than they're suddenly separated by a rude intrusion. Jumping on them both is a tall man with his shirt hanging out of his pants, the latest addition to their drunken group. Squinting, the man, whose name is John, ruffles Matthew's hair and shouts, "Way lad! Where's the drinks at?"

"The lad went to get the man who will keep my people drunk," Matthew says smirking. Lipstick is plastered across his face.

Laughing, John replies, "So where do I get myself a sassy piece of ass like this?"

Licking his lips, John tucks Marilyn's hair behind her ear. As drunk as he may be, almost instantly a huge rage builds inside of Matthew. Taking immediate offence to this blatant disrespectful action, Matthew pushes John away from Marilyn. Stunned as he was caught off guard, John holds out his hands and says, "Aye, I was just joking, lad."

Not hearing John's words as he's way too angry and drunk, Matthew charges at John. And, even in his intoxicated state, Matthew's aim is on point. Swinging his arm back he punches John directly in the eye. Falling to the floor with a thud, John hits his head on the floor. Without any hesitation, Matthew jumps on top of John and throws blow after blow at his head. Attempting to shield his face from the punches, John has his arms up high. Standing back, Marilyn is overseeing the attack and appears to be getting a thrill from watching Matthew beat John up. Little does she know, it's not for her benefit. After everything he has been through, Matthew has a short fuse and cannot bear to be disrespected. This unnecessary attack has nothing to do with Marilyn personally and everything to do with his perception of people's lack of loyalties. Unfortunately for John, his face is taking the brunt of every single person who has wronged Matthew.

Sitting in the corner overseeing what's taking place and unable to take any action are DCS Terry and DC Flores. Looking to her colleague DC Flores says, "Sir, shouldn't we stop this?"

DCS Terry calmly replies, "No."

"Sir, how can we not break this up?"

"For fuck's sake, Flores, if we go over there we'll blow our cover," Terry replies, rolling his eyes at her apparent stupidity.

"Yeah, but we can't just sit back and watch him beat this man to death."

"Don't worry, Flores, security will be along in a minute to split it up."

With her back to the unfolding attack, DC Flores says, "How can you be so sure?"

No sooner have the words left her mouth than DCS Terry nods his head towards the commotion. Looking over her shoulder, she sees the security guards rushing over. They instantly pull Matthew off his victim and four of them begin dragging him out of the venue. Throwing him out of the entrance one of the security guards shouts, "Go home, mate, and sleep it off."

Running out of the front entrance, Marilyn looks to the group of security guards, who are also her colleagues, and says, "That guy you've just thrown out, where did he go?"

The largest of the group, Dave, points towards the entrance of the alley way and says, "He's over there."

Looking across, Marilyn sees Matthew slumped on the pavement and out cold. Instantly believing the security team did this, she shouts, "Dave, what the fuck, man? What have you done to him?"

"Marz, you should know us by now, we didn't do that, he's just passed out from alcohol. Check him, he ain't got a scratch from us."

Running over to Matthew, Marilyn kneels down at the side of him. Checking his pulse, she instantly feels its presence, but it's weak.

Grabbing her phone, she calls for a taxi. Leaning into Matthew, Marilyn softly says into his ear, "Matthew, I'm getting us a taxi back to mine, is that okay with you?" Unable to make out his response, Marilyn repeats, "Matthew?"

Mumbling drunken words that make no sense under his breath, Matthew snuggles into Marilyn. No sooner has he tucked himself in, the taxi arrives.

It's past midnight and the search is complete. The worldwide web has done its job. Dorothy is sitting at her desk absorbing the reams of headlines that are linked to the name Evelyn Honey. She's overwhelmed by what she's seeing. She clicks the top link, which seems the most appropriate, and the page opens. The headline reads, *"Missing girl – Evelyn Jade Honey has been missing since 7 July – have you seen her?"*. There's an image next to the headline. Although Eve's hair is now dark, there is absolutely no getting away from the fact that she's the girl in the image. Dorothy is gobsmacked and feels physically sick – she knew something wasn't quite right. Keeping the tab open, she again conducts a search and clicks the next link. Opening a news article, Dorothy begins to scroll through it. Reading each individual word on the page and desperately trying to absorb the content, Dorothy works out that someone by the name of Matthew Honey has been charged with Evelyn's disappearance and potential murder and is undergoing an investigation with an upcoming trial. Continuing to scroll, Dorothy soon works out that Matthew Honey is Evelyn's true father and he's also facing a murder charge for his wife Lauren Honey.

Sitting back in her chair, Dorothy puts her hand over her mouth. She's in shock and doesn't know what to do next. Grabbing her mobile phone she dials 999, but just as she's about to hit the call button her inner voice stops her. Listening to this and trusting her gut instinct, she puts the phone down on the desk and continues her research. The next link she clicks brings her to a single landing web page. At the top in bold white letters against a black background it says, *"Have you seen my daughter?"* below this is the same image of the missing girl, Evelyn Jade Honey. Then, sitting just below the image is a mobile telephone number and the words, *"Help me find my daughter – call Matthew Honey."* Breathing deeply, Dorothy grabs her mobile, types in the number and this time she hits the call button.

At Marilyn's house, Matthew and Marilyn are upstairs in the bedroom. Having sobered up slightly, Matthew's wasting no time. He's wound up and highly frustrated. Receiving sexual satisfaction from this young female, Matthew's currently in heaven. The pair are enjoying some harmless naughty adult fun. Their clothes are sprawled out across the bedroom floor like a trail. Underneath the covers, Marilyn's giving Matthew a blowjob. His head sinking back into the pillow, Matthew's embracing the pleasure. She is sucking him from the bottom to the tip of his penis, whilst tickling his sensitive areas with her fingertips. Matthew thinks to himself that Marilyn is clearly experienced in the blowjob department and is loving this. He'd forgotten just how amazing this feels. As the sense of euphoria begins surging around his mind and body, Matthew desperately tries hard to hold back and not ejaculate too soon.

Sucking with passion, Marilyn circles her tongue around the tip of his penis. Kissing it, she then spits to lube it up and begins tugging at the tip. As the tip of Matthew's penis bounces off her lips, Matthew grabs the sheets and moans louder, feeling as if he's going to let go at any minute, Matthew has to surrender. Leaning down, he brings Marilyn up to the pillows. Wanting to last the night, he looks at Marilyn and whispers, "My turn."

Kissing her neck, Matthew makes his way down Marilyn's perky breasts and gently sucks her tiny nipples. She gyrates her hips in response, inviting Matthew to slip himself deep inside of her. Marilyn moans out loud. Seeing her embrace his touch makes Matthew get even harder than before. He's loving the taste of her skin. Using his tongue, Matthew licks his way down her stomach as he ventures down to her vaginal area. Loving the intimacy, Matthew touches her clitoris. Aware that Marilyn's enjoying the moment as much as he is, Matthew groans out loud as he feels her vagina is soaking wet. Working his way around her and seeing her legs shake as he touches a sensitive spot, Matthew's now ready to take the next step. Inserting one of his fingers inside her he says, "Oh God, you're so wet and tight."

Marilyn gyrates harder and harder. Inserting another two fingers, Matthew penetrates her deeply, whispering, "Are you ready for me?"

Moaning loudly Marilyn replies, "Yes, baby, give it to me, please."

"Oh, you want me to fuck you, do you?"

"Yes."

Loving the power he has, Matthew continues, "How bad do you want me to fuck you?"

"I'll do anything."

"Say please."

"Please, baby, just please fuck me."

Satisfied, Matthew responds, "Okay, just because you've been a good girl."

Grabbing the silver wrapper from off the bedside cabinet, Matthew opens this and rolls the condom down his erect penis.

"Are you ready for me?"

"Yes – please, please just put your dick inside me."

"Okay, I'm gonna give you what you want right now."

Matthew inserts his penis deep inside her. Marilyn begins moaning louder. Feeling her tight vagina wrapping around his girthy penis, Matthew begins banging hard against her. The rocking motion gets faster and faster, the bed violently hitting against the wall.

As Matthew enjoys this sexual act, he's oblivious to the fact that his phone is ringing in his pocket of his trousers. It's on silent, and with the bed banging loudly against the wall, and Marilyn's moaning, Matthew can't hear the phone vibrating. He's wrapped solely in the passionate moment and is completely unaware that he has missed five calls from the one person he has been waiting to speak to for months.

CHAPTER TWENTY-ONE

Maintain the Odds 7/7 at 7

It's late in the afternoon when Dorothy is awakened by her phone bleeping loudly across the room. She raises her head groggily from the arm of the sofa, on which she had once again passed out. Attempting to wake herself up, she staggers to the table to collect her phone and switch off the alarm. Squinting her eyes in the glare from the screen, Dorothy sees it isn't her alarm, it's a call from an unknown number. As she's about to press the accept button the call disconnects. Staggering back to the sofa, Dorothy slumps onto the cushions in her previous position, her phone now resting against her stomach. Lying back, she feels each throb of her head as it pounds from the copious amounts of alcohol she consumed last night. Placing her hand on the top of her head, she's tries to soothe the pain as pressure begins building up in her skull. She feels dizzy and nauseous. Dorothy's thoughts set off racing around her mind, taunting her. Recalling snippets of what she discovered online about Evelyn Honey, Dorothy feels unsure about what to do with this information. She knew something wasn't quite right, but now that she has the facts, she's keen to find out what the intentions of these people truly are before calling them out. Her phone begins to vibrate and this time she quickly answers the call. "Hello…"

A husky male voice at the other end says, "Who is this?"

"You're calling my phone. I'm sure you're supposed to know who I am, not the other way around," she snaps back.

"My name's Matthew Honey," the male voice replies abruptly. "Listen, you have left five missed calls on my phone and a voicemail stating you know where my daughter is. Is this some sort of sick joke to you? My life is not a game."

At the mention of his name, the penny drops and Dorothy begins to panic. She doesn't know what to say to this now angry man. "No, not at all. I'm glad you called back, Matthew." Sitting up and trying to wake herself properly, she continues, "Erm, I don't know how to say this, but I believe your daughter might be living at my daughter's house."

"What... Where? Tell me, and I'll be there right away. Who is she with – Jess, Jezebel?"

"Well, I don't really want to give out my daughter's address as there are other children in the house."

"You need to get those children out of that house NOW!" he shouts. "You don't understand what you've let in."

"What do you mean 'let in'?"

"Listen to me, you will lose every single one of those children."

"Matthew, you're scaring me."

There is a pause. Dorothy hears Matthew take a deep breath. When he speaks again his tone is lower. "Sorry, I don't mean to scare you. What's your name?"

"Dorothy."

"Dorothy, ah, that was my grandmother's name. So, listen, Dorothy, you don't want to tackle this situation alone, okay?"

"Erm, okay."

"What I need you to do is give me a location where we can meet up and we'll approach this together, is that alright? Honestly, there's no need to be afraid, I want to help."

"Thank you, Matthew. I think we should meet up in my local town centre."

"Okay, and where might that be, Dorothy?"

"Wythenshawe Civic Centre. Do you know it? It's in south Manchester."

She hears Matthew tapping on something, then, "Dorothy, is that near Manchester airport?"

"Yes, that's it."

"Right, so my GPS is saying I'm currently forty-five minutes away. I'm going to drive to you now."

"Okay, I'll get ready. There's a coffee shop in the middle of the town centre, I'll be waiting outside there. I've got red hair and will be wearing a black leather jacket."

"Okay, Dorothy, I'll see you soon." There is a slight pause, then Matthew says, "Oh, and Dorothy – make sure you don't tell anyone I'm on my way, okay?"

"Okay, I won't."

As he ends the call, Matthew's heart is racing. He has no clue what he's going to do when he sees his daughter, or Jess, for that matter. All he does know is he's going to ensure that he's armed and ready to take her back! His daughter will not be taken from him again. Reaching inside his trouser pocket, he pulls out what he thinks is the cross from Reverend Andrew Read, but when he looks in his hand, he sees it's actually the heart-shaped locket. Taking a deep breath in, Matthew tries to stay in control of his emotions. He had completely forgotten that he had this. Not wanting to look at the tainted trinket, and paranoid that it might somehow be feeding information back to the sadistic owner, Matthew wraps the bloodstained bandage from his hand around it and shoves it back inside his trouser pocket. Reaching inside his other pocket, this time he pulls out the cross from Reverend Andrew. Kissing it, he prays internally for support and protection. He then says out loud, "I need you now more than ever."

Putting the cross inside the internal pocket on his jacket so that it is resting against his heart, Matthew is ready! Pulling out of his parking space, he sets off on what is hopefully his final journey without his daughter.

It's past three in the afternoon and Lewis is just waking up, hung-over. His arms around Eve, he is deep in thought whilst she's sleeping. Placing his hand on her stomach, he still cannot believe the life-changing news. A life is being created inside of Eve. But not just any life– his own little miracle. The thought of becoming a dad at the young age of sixteen truly scares him. He has no clue how his mum is going to react to the news and he hasn't even thought about how he will financially support his child. All he does know is he's one hundred percent going to be there every single day for his prince or princess.

Lewis breathes in the scent of Eve's hair. He's so in love with her. As Lewis kisses Eve on the neck, she slowly begins to wake. Looking over her shoulder, she says in her quiet morning voice, "Hello, cheeky." Kissing him, she continues, "So, you're still here, then?"

"Of course I'm here, where else would I be?"

"Thought you might have tried to disappear in the night. Don't worry, though, I'd have found you."

Smiling, he replies, "Look, don't get me wrong, I totally thought about it, but how could I just abandon you both? I haven't got a dad anymore – there is no way my child is growing up without a dad. And your mum not being around... I'm sure you'll never let our child be without his or her mum, will you?"

"Never! This child, our baby, I will forever protect." Turning her body, Eve continues, "Look me in the eyes, Lewis."

"Why...?"

"Just do it."

"Okay."

"Should anything go wrong, and I mean anything, promise me, no matter what, you will put our child before anything or anyone?"

"Eve, that's a given."

"Even me."

"What do you mean 'even you'?"

"Just promise me."

"Eve, you're making me nervous. What do you mean 'even you', where you going?"

"Lewis, there's a lot you don't know about me and you'll never know about me. I don't know my eternal fate, I just know I have no choice, I'm stuck. Should you ever have to choose, choose our child."

Feeling more and more confused by the second, Lewis says, "Eve, baby, where's this coming from?"

"Please, Lewis, don't ask questions, just tell me that you'll always put our baby first."

"Okay, okay, I promise, I will put our child before anyone, even you."

"I will take you with me, but I don't know what the end result is going to be for us all. If I change and those who want me come after me, please save our baby."

Baffled, Lewis says, "Eve, maybe I should get you something to drink?"

Saying no more, Eve cups Lewis's face in her hands and stares intently at him. Their eyes lock together and Lewis drifts into a trance, frozen stiff...

She wants to know whether her nightly visits have been effective, whether Lewis's soul has accepted its fate. She delves deep into Lewis's inner existence. Almost instantly, she gains full reign over his sight and his mind. Satisfied that her hauntings in the night are taking effect, she gazes through the windows of his soul. Travelling deeper and deeper, she sees Lewis's spiritual essence is, as she hoped, trapped. The evil she has planted within has taken rule. Her premeditated possession has overpowered Lewis's soul. The dark entity lurking inside this young boy's physical form is patiently waiting for her final command. Only then will this destructive energy surface. Content with her findings, she slowly retreats from his mind...

Choking, Lewis shakes his head. "What was that?"

"What...?"

Still coughing slightly, Lewis continues, "I feel like I just blacked out."

"Don't know what you're talking about."

Confusion spreading fast across his face, but not wanting to create any sort of rift between him and the soon-to-be mother of his child, Lewis says, "Oh, erm, probably nothing, then."

With a somewhat deceitful expression upon her face, Eve playfully replies, "You're silly sometimes, Lewis, but also soft and caring. These are the things I love about you the most. Never lose that."

Smiling, he tucks Eve's hair behind her ear, gazing at her as he says, "You're so beautiful. We're going to have one good-looking kid, thanks to you."

Blushing she replies, "You're not so bad yourself, Mr Parkinson."

Feeling slightly weird as he's not been called this before and the last person he heard referred to by that name was his dad, Lewis decides to get off the lovey-dovey subject before he really does show his soft side and burst out crying. Breathing deeply and pulling away he says, "Come on, let's go civic. I think we should cook dinner for everyone this evening. We need to sort our chef skills now that we're going to be parents. Don't you have to, like, cook actual food for them?"

Laughing, Eve replies, "Yes, Lew, you have to cook actual food for children, but we've got plenty of time for that."

"Well, let's just get out the house for a bit, then. I'll message the lads, see if they fancy a civic trip."

"Sure, let me just get dressed."

Leaning over and kissing Eve on the head, Lewis smiles. As he turns to get off the bed, he becomes tangled in the covers. He makes a desperate bid to save himself but it's too late, and he falls off the edge of the bed. Eve howls with laughter. Completely tickled by what has just happened, she rolls round the bed, chuckling loudly. A few seconds later, Lewis manages to free himself from the entrapment of the bedsheets and jumps up. He's in a fluster and his hair is sticking up. Looking across at Eve and hearing her beautiful laughter, he too begins belly laughing. Wiping the tears from her face, Eve says, "You absolute wally!"

Putting his head down as he continues to chuckle, Lewis shakes his head. "I know, but that's why you like me enough to have a baby with me."

Raising his eyebrows in a cheeky manner, Lewis gives her one final smirk and then makes his way out of the room, leaving Eve to continue cackling away to herself as he closes the bedroom door.

Lewis is met by Jesse in the hallway. He is completely unsure if he should approach Jesse about Eve's current situation. Not feeling brave enough, instead of speaking out, Lewis decides to simply smile at Jesse and then put his head down. But then Jesse speaks. "So, Eve told me that you now know of her situation." Sternly looking Lewis in the eye, Jesse continues, "You're ready to be a father now then, Lewis?"

Lewis was not expecting this to be Jesse's opening statement. "Erm, yes, I suppose I am," he replies. Lifting his head and attempting to be a big man, Lewis looks Jesse in the eye and continues, "Jesse, I haven't got a dad, as you know. I do not want the same for my child. I promise I will forever look after Eve. Yes, I'm scared, who wouldn't be at sixteen, but I won't give up. Wherever they go, I'll be there."

Smirking, Jesse simply replies, "I know you will. There's no getting away now, Lewis, your fate is aligned."

Just then, Jesse is distracted by the sounds of Freddie, Terence and Rupert who are roughhousing downstairs. Jesse says nothing further and slowly makes his way down the staircase. Relieved as he has just escaped a very awkward conversation, Lewis goes into the bathroom and locks the door.

Lewis places a hand on either side of the sink. He has no clue who to turn to or what to actually do. The only person he wants advice from right now is his dad. Closing his eyes, he whispers, "Dad, why did you have to go?"

Without an answer to his question, Lewis opens his eyes and turns on the tap. Steam flows up, clouding the mirror on the cabinet above the sink. Splashing the water on his face, Lewis gasps as it almost burns his skin but at the same time wakes him up. Examining his reflection, he silently assesses his ability to be a good dad, or in fact, a dad at all. Looking himself directly in the eye, Lewis is psyching himself up for the unknown.

As he continues to stare at his reflection intently, the steam flowing up and the hot water gushing down the plughole, the energy within the bathroom suddenly changes and Lewis feels as if he's no longer alone. A pungent stench manifests and circulates inside his nostrils, hitting the back of his throat, making him gag. His stomach churns as this vile taste grows stronger and stronger. Wanting to run, Lewis discovers his legs are frozen. From nowhere, Lewis hears a familiar nursery rhyme tune. He closes his eyes and wiggles his finger inside his eardrum, but no matter how hard he tries to get rid of the sound, the repetitive rhyming song continues on a loop. As it gets louder and louder, Lewis suddenly hears, "Your soul is mine..."

No sooner have the words travelled into his mind than a huge bolt of intense pain shoots through his eyeballs. Screaming out and quickly opening his eyes, he looks at his reflection in the mirror and sees that his eyes have turned jet-black. Not a hint of his natural colour or white can be seen. Not only this, his intuition was right – he's not alone. She's back! The taller of the two demonic entities from his nightmares is standing right behind him.

Unlike Lewis, her eyes are blood red. Her body is lacerated with black rips, the wounds oozing a sinister thick black substance. As he attempts to adjust his sight to the image before him, Lewis's skin turns a deep shade of grey matching the image of this evil entity. Feeling an excruciating pain all over his body, Lewis screams out as rips erupt across his flesh. The transition is horrific. Seemingly pleased with his transformation, the demonic figure places her finger to her mouth and mimes, "Sshh..."

Apparently satisfied, she suddenly disappears. Lewis's soul is released, for now. Falling to the ground and choking, Lewis curls up on the tiled floor and gasps for air. Feeling as though he's dying, he places his hands over his face. Lewis experiences a pins and needles sensation in his eyeballs. This same pain then travels around his body. But no sooner has it started than the pain magically begins to ease. Still gripped by anxiety, feeling as if he's losing his mind, Lewis is struggling to understand why this is happening to him. Slowly regaining his strength, he looks to his hands and sees that they're no longer grey. Feeling relieved to have full control over his body once again, but still weak and struggling to catch his breath, he slowly pulls himself up with the support of the sink and turns off the tap. As the steam clears a bit, Lewis hesitantly looks in the mirror. He wipes away some of the condensation. Thankfully, his reflection looking back is normal. He's no longer grey and his eyes are back to their normal shade. Adrenaline surging throughout his body and his senses on high alert, Lewis is a nervous wreck. He places his hand gently around his throat. His breathing is becoming somewhat erratic and he desperately tries to regulate it once more. Overcome with anxiety, this young lad suddenly feels as if he's about to faint. Hearing a bang on the door, Lewis jumps.

He hears Freddie shout through the bathroom door, "Lewis, is that you? Are you okay in there?"

Jumping with fright, Lewis knocks the pot containing the whole family's toothbrushes off the side of the sink. The ceramic pot smashes into multiple pieces on the floor. His heart racing at one hundred miles an hour, Lewis tries to say something to reassure his brother, but the words won't come out. All he can do right now is make growling noises as he tries to clear his throat. Hearing muffled voices coming from outside the bathroom door, Lewis curls up on the floor. As he catches his breath, Lewis's adrenaline levels slowly deplete to a semi-normal level.

He hears another knock on the door and this time Eve shouts, "Lew, you okay?"

"Yeah, sorry," Lewis replies hoarsely. "Tell Freddie I was just choking on some water. I'll be right out."

Feeling weak and swaying slightly, he sits on the toilet to catch his breath. Gathering his thoughts, Lewis cannot help but become confused as he begins to question why these traumatising episodes keep happening to him. Questioning his sanity, Lewis gets ready to leave the bathroom. As he stands he looks back into the mirror. Other than a lot of condensation, all is as it should be.

No sooner has a huge sense of relief sunk in than something begins to change. Squinting his eyes, Lewis sees the following appearing in the condensation on the mirror: "7/7 at 7". He unlocks the bathroom door, rips it open and bursts out onto the landing, almost knocking over Eve who is standing right outside the door.

Matthew waits nervously in the coffee shop for the woman with red hair and a black leather jacket, but she is nowhere to be seen. His hands are shaking and he almost tips the cappuccino he has just ordered. Suddenly his phone dings and he jumps. This time he does tip the hot drink over himself. Not caring about the soaking wet patch burning away on his pants, Matthew pulls his phone out of his pocket. He sees it's a text from Marilyn: *Where did you go? I had fun last night, you wanna do it again tonight? M x.*

Frustrated that it wasn't Dorothy, and not wanting to get involved with anything else right now, Matthew deletes the message and puts his phone on the table. He breathes deeply, feeling sick with worry and nerves. No sooner has he allowed these emotions to take full reign over his mind, his inner critical voice begins feeding him destructive and cruel words.

"Ha! You thought she was going to help you... How stupid do you feel? Help you? Pfft, who'd want to help you? Hang your head in shame, Matthew Honey. You don't deserve help, you don't deserve your daughter back. Why don't you go and do the world a favour and kill yourself?"

Trying not to get agitated, and desperate to distract himself from the taunting words, Matthew takes in his surroundings. There are people everywhere. From newborn babies in prams to elderly people with supportive walking apparatus, this town centre has a vast range of personalities. Each person is rushing around at their maximum capacity, as though they're running short on time. Holding bag, after bag, after bag, they're all juggling their items. From single people to loved up couples, to huge oversized families, and all the bits in between, Matthew's eyes are seeing it all. Hearing shouting coming from behind him, Matthew turns to see a kick-off between two individuals. Not wanting to get involved, he quickly turns and picks up his phone. Not a single missed call or message. With a great big sigh, Matthew's almost ready to accept defeat and leave. While he watches the moving bodies surrounding him, Matthew fails to notice two people who are watching his every move.

Across the way, camped up in a cosy homerun café with a clear visual of Matthew are DCS Terry and DC Flores. Slurping back his cheap instant coffee and pulling a face, DCS Terry says to his colleague, "Urgh!" Wiping his mouth and hoping the bitter taste of cheap coffee will disappear, he continues, "So, what do we think this is about?"

"I have no clue, but this guy can travel." With an I'm-tired-of-this-job expression upon her face, she continues, "Exactly how many locations have we been to in the past… how many days?"

"I don't know, Flores, but this one's got to be the best location by far for people watching." Nodding his head, he begins laughing as a male and female openly begin arguing in the middle of the small but extremely busy town centre. "Look at that – no one's even battin' an eye lid." The female suddenly swings for the male with her fist and hits him in the head. DCS Terry bursts out laughing and says, "Go on, girl!"

"Stop staring, it's not very professional," Flores says.

"Listen, I've done my research on this town. They used to film a reality-style talk show and I read that the producers of the show never had a problem finding local "talent" let's say to appear on the programme. Honestly, Flores, don't worry, this lot love an audience."

"Oh, behave yourself, old man."

"Who you callin' old man, cheeky? I'm not old, I'm experienced."

Winking, DCS Terry once again sets off sniggering under his breath as the kick-off continues. Shaking her head, DC Flores gives in and smiles back at him as she too drinks her cheap instant coffee. Getting back to the task in hand and being the great efficient Detective Constable that she is, DC Flores says, "Shall we set up the camera just in case?"

"Just in case what?"

"Well, you never know – it looks like he may be meeting someone." DCS Terry stares with a blank expression on his face. DC Flores continues, "Don't tell me you haven't noticed how nervous he is? The man keeps checking his phone. Something seems, I don't know, different…"

Pulling a face as he hasn't been paying even the slightest bit of attention to what Matthew Honey is up to, DCS Terry smirks back at her. Distracted from the task in hand, DCS Terry's current focus is one hundred percent on the entertaining kick-off just outside the café window. DCS Terry's not fussed about the cameras one bit. At present, his only concern is whether he has to move, and so he says in a lazy tone, "Does it require my assistance, Flores?"

"No," she says, rolling her eyes. "I just need you to keep watch and let me know if you see anything of interest to record. Is that okay or too much work for you?"

Laughing under his breath he says, "Can we record this kickoff?"

DC Flores frowns. Her eyes say it all.

"Okay, fine, have it your way. As long as I don't have to move, that'll do for me. Crack on then, Flores."

Matthew continues to check his phone every thirty seconds or so. He's extremely anxious and is now completely unsure about the woman he spoke to today. Will Dorothy show up? Is this woman genuine or is this a cruel prank? With his faith firmly placed with the powers that be, Matthew tries to ignore the niggling voice taunting him inside his mind.

"Ha ha! See, I told you she wasn't coming. Try speaking over me all you like, you know I'm right. She's not going to help you. Just like the rest, you've been lured into a trap. She's probably sat with a group laughing at you right now! Watching as you keep checking your phone. Go on, do it, go and kill yourself. Actually, why don't you take a few people down with you? Yeah, let's have some fun first. You're going to die, so why not."

The clock is ticking, the day is almost coming to an end – it's now reaching evening time. Too anxious to sit back and do nothing and wanting to stop the voices in his head, Matthew decides he's not waiting any longer. He reaches for his phone. This time he's not messing around. He gets Dorothy's number up and hits the call button. No sooner has it begun to ring in his ear than Matthew hears a loud ringtone coming from behind him. Suddenly it stops and he hears a woman's voice say, "Hello."

With a confused expression spread upon his face, Matthew looks over his shoulder. As he turns, he sees an older trendy looking woman with beautiful red hair and a black leather jacket walking towards him with her phone to her ear. Making eye contact, Matthew says, "Dorothy?"

"Yes."

Matthew stands, his hand shaking as he puts it out to her. Returning the gesture, Dorothy shakes his hand. She places her phone on the table and holds his hand inside both of hers. She smiles at him with an expression of sincerity and love as she says, "It's all okay." Taking a seat, Dorothy calmly says, "It's good to finally meet you, Matthew, and please accept my sincerest apologies for ringing you so many times last night. I'd had a drink, you see."

"Please don't be sorry," Matthew replies, his voice a little shaky with nerves. "I've developed somewhat of an evening drinking habit myself."

Looking down at the table, Matthew fumbles with a tiny piece of paper to distract himself. Under the table, his leg bounces up and down. Her eyes falling on Matthew's fidgeting leg, Dorothy says, "So, did you find the place easily, Matthew?"

"Yeah, erm, my sat nav just brought me straight here."

"Oh, right. If you don't mind me asking, where were you?"

"I was in, erm, I think it's called Chester…"

"Oh, yes, I know Chester, there's a huge beautiful racecourse there."

Smiling and temporarily putting down the tiny piece of paper he's fiddling with, Matthew says, "Yeah, I went last night. Both my horses won big and I got a bit too drunk whilst celebrating. They kicked me out in the end."

"Oh, dear, that does sound like an eventful night."

Smiling and huffing slightly as she doesn't know the half of it, Matthew bites the bullet and tells the truth. After all, what's he got to lose?

"To be honest, I've gone off the rails since I lost Evelyn Jade."

Looking relieved at his mention of Evelyn Jade, Dorothy asks, "If you don't mind me asking, what's your story, Matthew?" Pausing for a brief second, Dorothy then says, "I mean, I read some bits online about you, but, I mean you can't always believe what these things say."

"My story? Huh. Well, Dorothy, how long have you got?"

"Believe it or not, all night."

Matthew takes a deep breath in and releases it with a huge sigh. He doesn't know where to begin. "What would you like to know?"

"Well, where it all... erm... What... Erm... Okay, sorry, let me start again. So, online it said something about your wife and your daughter."

"Yeah, believe it or not, Dorothy, I once had it all. Smart clothes, successful business, loving wife, beautiful daughter, family home – you name it, I had it. I was rich with love and money." Laughing slightly and looking down at his current appearance, Matthew continues, "Huh, now look at me. No family, no business, living out of a car and hunting the unknown. Grabbing any tiny snippet I can to piece together a tainted trail made by the impure. Ha, my how the journey of life can dramatically change."

"You said something on the phone earlier that got me thinking, and, well, if I'm honest, you actually scared me. You said I will lose all the children. What did you mean by that?"

"Dorothy, I don't want to scare you – the last thing I want to do is scare you. I want to help you. But, if that is my daughter you have living with your family and the entity who has stolen her soul, then we really need to act quickly."

"Sorry, what did you just say?"

"I know it makes no sense to you right now and I honestly don't know how to defeat this demonic entity, but I promise you this: I will happily sacrifice myself in order to save the souls of our young."

"Matthew, without being too judgemental, and please forgive me if I sound blunt, but, there's no such thing as demons."

"Huh, yeah that's what I once thought. Lemme ask you this – have you been experiencing nightmares?"

Dorothy looks shocked. She hesitantly replies, "Yes."

"Okay, so have you noticed any strange behavioural changes in the children?"

Closing her eyes she says, "Yes, my granddaughter Hope is currently in hospital with my daughter as they both stopped breathing."

"Stopped breathing!" It's more serious than he thought. Matthew tries to calm himself slightly as he continues, "Erm, anything else?"

"Yes." Again, she pauses, as if she's reluctant to tell him something. Breathing deeply, Dorothy quietly whispers, "I watched as Hope's eyes turned black and she went grey."

Matthew's jaw drops. He has been waiting for this day for months and now that it's here he has no clue how to process this information. Remaining in shock, he says, "Oh my goodness, Dorothy. Not to panic you, but I truly believe this is Jezebel and my daughter."

Suddenly, overwhelmed by the facts he has just been fed, Matthew's chest has gone tight and his head begins to spin. He has been waiting for this day for such a long time and he truly didn't believe he'd ever get his wish. Throwing himself back against the chair, Matthew goes slightly limp and holds his chest.

"Matthew, Matthew, Matthew, are you okay?" Dorothy asks, panicked. There is no response, so she shouts to one of the girls cleaning the table across the way, "Excuse me, can we have some water, please?" Grabbing the glass of water from the waitress when she brings it, Dorothy presses it against Matthew's lips. "Here, sip this."

Taking tiny amounts at a time, as the colour returns to his cheeks and he regains control, Matthew says, "I'm sorry. I've been waiting for this day for, well, a year now." Checking his phone he sees it is six in the evening and the date is the seventh of the seventh, "Actually, it's a year to the date. Please… erm… don't… Crap… Dorothy, I believe if you're going to lose your loved ones, then it could potentially be tonight."

"WHAT?!" Dorothy shouts. "Hang on, we don't even know if it is your daughter – and who is Jezebel?"

"Jezebel is the demonic entity who has stolen my daughter's soul and has a sick impure intention to unleash upon us all. She's doing this by using the souls of the young and the vulnerable."

"Well, there you go, I don't know a Jezebel."

"Can I ask who is with my daughter?"

"Eve has moved in with her dad, Jesse. There is no Jezebel in my daughter's house."

"Does your daughter have an ex-husband, or is the children's dad around?"

"No, Phil died over a year ago. I've only just found out that he took his own life."

"Oh, I'm sorry to hear that. That's very sad. Please accept my sincere condolences. Suicide is terrible. Believe me, I've contemplated it enough. It's only because Eve is still living that I haven't, you know, ended it all." He is trying to empathise with Dorothy and doesn't want to seem heartless, but Matthew is aware that, should his predication be correct, he's on a very slim time limit. "Can I ask if Jesse looks like... Phil, did you say?"

"Yes, it's Phil. Erm, well, I don't think I've..." Dorothy pauses for a moment. Then, as if something has just clicked into place in her brain she continues, "Yes, he does look like Phil. I never really noticed it before."

"Dorothy, I'm sorry, I know this is the last thing you want to hear, but that's how this demon does what it does so quickly. It preys on broken homes and takes the form of the missing parent to get into the home quickly and without question."

Dorothy looks as though she is struggling to process what Matthew is saying to her.

"What do we do?"

Reaching out and holding her hands, Matthew breathes deeply as he says, "Dorothy, I really don't know, but as I said, I will happily die trying to stop this sadistic entity from taking our young."

Looking to Matthew, Dorothy says, "So we pray for answers?"

Overseeing the events taking place, DCS Terry and DC Flores are recording the footage of Matthew and the unknown woman.

Suddenly DCS Terry spots something of huge interest, "Quick, give me that camera, Flores."

She passes it over and DCS Terry begins filming a group of young people heading in the direction of the café window. Within this group is a young male and a young female who have their arms around one another. Peering through the lens on the camera, DCS Terry says, "I don't believe…"

"What, sir?" DC Flores asks. Getting no response she repeats, "You don't believe what?"

Dropping the camera on the table, DCS Terry rushes out of the café. He looks around but the whole group, including the young male and female, have all disappeared. DC Flores appears from the café holding all their belongings in her arms. "Sir, what is it?"

"I swear that was…" Scratching his head, DCS Terry continues, "Can we rewind on that thing?"

"Yes sir, why?"

"I need to watch something back, come on." Checking to see that Matthew is still sat at the coffee shop engrossed in conversation with the unknown woman, DCS Terry heads back inside the café with DC Flores. Sitting back at the table by the window, he says, "Rewind that for me."

"How far?"

"I don't know – five minutes or so should do it."

Rewinding the footage, they both begin watching intently. DC Flores has no clue what she's searching for and yet DCS Terry is on high alert for what he has just seen. Suddenly he shouts, "There! Stop the footage." DC Flores pauses the footage, struggling to see what he's seeing. Continuing he says, "Zoom in on her there."

Zooming in and bringing the image closer to her face, the realisation sinks in. DC Flores says, "Oh my goodness."

"Yes, is that who I think it is?"

"Sir, I believe so."

"That's fucking Evelyn Jade Honey!"

They both sit back in their seats, trying to process what they've just captured. This was the last thing they thought they'd find when they started this assignment. Now, they both have no clue what to do next. Looking across to Matthew through the window, they are gobsmacked. Staring back at his colleague, DCS Terry says, "So the bastard was telling the truth all along. She's alive."

CHAPTER TWENTY-TWO

Expand the Empire

The hands on the clocks are striking loudly one after the other. Every tick and tock can be heard echoing throughout the empty corridors of Wythenshawe Hospital. It is just past six thirty in the evening on the seventh of July. Alice and baby Hope are sleeping in their beds. Inside their room, the bleeping from the machines, which they are both hooked up to, sounds louder than normal alongside the deafening silence. The genius inventions are taking both Alice and Hope's vital observations at thirty-minute intervals.

The specialists who were flown in specifically to find out what is taking Alice's life and making baby Hope so poorly were left scratching their heads. They got no closer today than they did yesterday to figuring it out.

Though the welfare of their sick patients is the biggest priority, the hospital staff are having issues of their own. The vast majority are in deep mourning. The bodies of their colleagues Zander, Jack and Emily have been found in the laboratory, having been brutally killed on the hospital grounds. Without any answer to how these horrific and sickening murders occurred, all the staff are anxious, afraid and overcome by a deep internal sadness. With no suspect, motive, or CCTV evidence, Wythenshawe Hospital remains on high alert. Nervous about falling victim to another unprovoked attack, but aware that the show must go on, the staff must still tend to their poorly patients. A huge decision has been undertaken. Due to the graphic disturbing nature of the three murders and the need to put the safety of everyone, both staff and patients, first, the powers that be have decided they have no choice but to place the building on lock down. No visitors are permitted to be on the hospital grounds. This has never happened before.

The corridors are empty. The hospital is extremely quiet and has an eerie vibration circulating throughout. In fact, it's so unnerving that the overworked hospital staff, who are more often than not on the brink of insanity due to upheaval and stress of visiting hour, would now love nothing more than to have the chaotic distraction.

Inside Alice and Hope's room, darkness is upon the sleeping pair. The blinds are closed and the windows along with the doors are shut tight. All appears as it should be. Both Alice and Hope are dreaming, locked inside their minds. An unexpected energy develops within the room and begins blowing the helium-filled balloons alongside the curtains. As if feeling a chill, Alice shivers under the bedsheets. With her eyes closed tight she can smell something disgusting.

The sinister breeze has not entered the room alone. A dark manifestation is making its presence known. Fierce, relentless and unnerving, this powerful energy immediately takes over the room, and a grey mist begins to seep inside. No sooner has this cunning manifestation formed than it initiates its mission. It travels across the room to the door. Wrapping around the handle, the mist travels inside the keyhole. The lock is turned. Now no one can get in or out of the room.

Becoming agitated, Alice is now able to move. She fights against the bedsheets and begins moaning out loud in her sleep, "No, no, no, don't take them..."

The mist elegantly travels up the frame of Alice's bed. Starting at her toes, it slowly wraps itself around her entire body. Securing itself tightly, it restricts Alice from making any movements should she wake. Ready, the deceitful element now calls for its owner. A gentle humming begins and the sound of "Ring a' Ring o' Roses" can be heard. Getting louder, the humming turns into singing.

Suddenly the walls begin to tremor. They give a final shake and… she's back!

Standing at the end of Alice's bed is Jezebel. She's ready to play one final game and take what she believes is rightfully hers. Jezebel stares intently at Alice through the gap in her hair. Her smile is deceitful. Embracing the vision, Jezebel enters Alice's mind. She begins to turn her dream into a sickening, traumatic nightmare. As Jezebel's premeditated horrific events begin to manifest inside her dream, Alice's pulse and heartrate go wild. An error flashes up on the machine she is hooked up to, triggering the alarm. The lines on the readout rapidly become out of sync and erratic. In the bed alongside Alice, Hope's reading suddenly flatlines. With no heartrate or pulse, the monitors show that this baby girl is no longer alive.

There are sounds of panic coming from just outside the door as the nurses on duty frantically pull at the handle in a desperate bid to enter the room. Ignoring the commotion outside the room, Jezebel remains at the end of Alice's bed. Placing one grey wounded foot in front of the other, she slowly makes her way towards Hope's cot. Reaching inside, she grabs the precious little girl. Holding her newest addition to her demonic empire tightly in her arms, she whispers, "Ring a' Ring o' Roses – your soul is mine. Ring a' Ring o' Roses – welcome to the dark side."

As these familiar trigger words circulate inside Hope's tiny mind, her observation machine continues to flatline. Whispering one final time, Jezebel says, "Your soul is mine…"

Almost instantly Hope's eyes shoot open. No longer resembling that of the human race, her eyes are jet-black. Embracing her new form, baby Hope isn't making a single sound. This baby girl's soul has accepted its fate. Tainted and impure, her skin tone changes to grey. She's mirroring the image of her new owner. Proud of her newest addition, Jezebel raises baby Hope high and, as she screams out, the black substance gushes from her mouth. Basking in the glory of her latest victory, Jezebel ingests the black substance seeping from Hope's body. Their DNA has now become one.

As the staff continue to bang at the door, Jezebel makes her way back across to Alice. With full control over Alice's nightmare, Jezebel launches her final game as she leads Alice into the darkest depths of her own mind.

Alice is surrounded by darkness. Looking straight ahead, she sees a single door. Suddenly, the door creaks open. Shaking from head to toe and with nowhere else to go, Alice slowly makes her way towards it. The only sound she can hear is that of her own breath as it leaves her body. She closes her eyes as she walks through the doorway. As soon as she's through, the door slams shut! Jumping and turning around, Alice hears a click as the door locks. Feeling sick to her stomach, Alice sees a spotlight in the distance. She bravely takes one step after another and heads towards the light.

Alice gasps loudly as she sees a woman swinging from the ceiling with a rope around her neck. Rushing to her aid, Alice shouts, "Help! Help! Someone help me!"

As she reaches the swinging body, Alice slips in a huge pool of thick red blood. Traumatised, she screams as she looks to her hands. They're covered in the woman's blood and her clothes are also soaked. Peering up, she sees the hanging body slowly begin to swing round.

Remaining on the ground, Alice crawls backwards. She's desperately trying get out of the puddle of blood, and as far away as possible from the hanging corpse. With her eyes fixated on the deceased woman, Alice is terrified. She feels at any moment this woman is going to spring to life and chase after her. Alice's heart is beating so fast it feels as if it's going to pop! As the corpse twists round on the rope and she sees the woman's face, her jaw drops. The body hanging from the thick coarse rope – is her! No sooner have her eyes taken in the realities of this horrific vision than the thick red blood she's covered in suddenly turns black. Feeling sick and franticly trying to escape, Alice throws herself forward.

Opening her eyes, Alice finds she is soaking wet from head to toe and inexplicably back in her bed at her home. Attempting to catch her breath, she touches her head and body to ensure she's in one piece. Relief begins to sink in, but as Alice takes a true look around her bedroom, she becomes extremely confused. The room is not the way she left it. It's dark and cold, and a thick grey mist is coating the floor.

A huge bang and a loud squawk comes from the window, making Alice jump and yell out. The curtains are closed. Not knowing if she should run a mile or see what the noise was, Alice decides to be brave and investigate further. She slowly clambers off the bed, leaving her sheets trailing behind her and heads to the window. Her eyes focused and breathing deeply, Alice pulls back the curtains. Much to her relief, there's nothing and no one there.

Turning back to the room, she sees that the mist has expanded. It's now so thick she can barely make out what's in front of her. Once again a loud bang comes from the window, along with an intense squawk. Looking over her shoulder, this time Alice sees a huge black Raven standing on her window ledge. The evil-looking creature stares at her with bright red eyes. Freaked out and making a run for it, Alice trips over the bedsheets as she rushes to get out of the room. Dragging herself up onto her feet, she doesn't so much as glance back as she's desperate to escape. She grabs the doorknob and flings the door open. Bursting out of her room, Alice sees the mist has taken over the hallway, too. Unable to hold it in any longer, she begins crying hysterically. She's so scared and has no clue what is going on. Alice bites the bullet and shouts, "Jesse…? Lewis…? Mum…?"

Hearing no response, she takes one step forward and heads towards the stairway. The silence throughout is deafening. Alice is on edge. She keeps feeling as if someone is standing behind her, but each time she jumps and looks over her shoulder, she sees there's no one there. Relived but also feeling as if she is losing the plot, Alice continues to walk forward. What she doesn't realise is that now someone *is* standing behind her. No sooner has she turned her head forward than a dark demonic figure appears from out of the mist. Oblivious to this, Alice cautiously continues. With a huge desire to hear someone else's voice, again Alice shouts, "Jesse, Lewis, this isn't funny. Where are you?" Still getting no response she shouts, "Hello…?"

The floorboards creak. Alice jumps and peers over her shoulder. Yet again, there's no one standing there. Closing her eyes, Alice finally arrives at the stairway. Breathing deeply and opening her eyes once more, she sees her sons standing on the stairs. Frantic, she shouts, "Oh my God, my boys!"

Not so much as a flinch comes from the boys. They all remain frozen stiff. As she raises her hand to her mouth, a single tear rolls down her face. She's so scared. Taking in the disturbing vision before her eyes, as the dark mist continues to take over, Alice can see each one of her sons standing on a step. They're all positioned in age order, youngest at the bottom. Desperate to get them to come to her but not wanting to disturb whoever or whatever is present inside the house with them, Alice whispers, "Freddie… Terence… Rupert… Lewis… mummy's here."

Staring intently, she sees, yet again, that they've all not so much as flinched. And, what's even more disturbing, they're all facing the wall. At a loss as to what to do next, she prays to get a response from her first born. Her voice shaking as fear takes over, Alice again whispers, "Lewis…?"

Focused on the traumatising image in front of her, Alice doesn't attempt to look back. Instead she takes one step down the stairway, shaking from head to toe. The only sound Alice can hear is that of her heart beating as it pulsates rapidly throughout her body. Arriving on the step next to where Lewis is positioned, Alice reaches out and touches his shoulder. "Lewis?"

As she turns him to face her, she instantly screams out at this horrific image of her first born child. Lewis has transformed and has taken a true demonic form. His eyes are jet-black. As soon as she screams, each of her sons turn, one after the other. Each of them mirror the same horrific image. Alice's heart feels as if at any moment it will burst. Traumatised, she shouts at the top of her voice, "Wake up, Alice, wake the fuck up!"

Alice's eyes are drawn to the darkness at the bottom of the staircase. Standing there holding baby Hope is a dark demonic figure of a woman, her eyes are bright red and she has long hair which is jet-black. Her skin is grey and covered in wounds that ooze black liquid. Gazing at Alice through the gap in her hair, the terrifying figure screams out. Alice turns to run back up the staircase and comes face to face with… Eve. But not Eve as she knows her. This version of Eve mirrors the appearance of her sons, her skin an unearthly grey and gaping black holes for eyes. Eve hits out and pushes Alice down the stairs. Falling at high speed and hitting her head on the door, Alice is knocked on conscious.

When Alice awakens, her brain is throbbing inside of her skull, she sees a thick puddle of deep red blood on the floor. Reaching around the back of her head, Alice touches the tender area. She brings her hand out in front of her and sees it is coated in the same thick red blood. Shaking, Alice sits up. She looks down at her clothes, which are also soaked in her own blood. Unsure about what has happened to her and wondering where her sons are, Alice frantically looks to the stairway. They're no longer there. All four boys have gone. Peering back at the floor, she sees six individual trails of a black substance smeared across the floor. Lifting herself, in pain, Alice decides to follow this. With every step she takes, her surroundings are getting darker and darker. Following the trail leads her towards the dining room. As she reaches the doorway, she sees the room is pitch black. Holding her head in her hand, she says, "Lewis…?"

But the only sound Alice can hear is the echo from her own voice. Weakened, she slumps to the floor. Her head spinning and her energy levels depleting from the blood loss, Alice's body is becoming frail with every second that passes. She's almost ready to surrender when a light unexpectedly appears in the dining room. Her eyes are barely open, she looks into the room and sees that the space is no longer pure. There are no pictures on the wall. The room is dark, eerie and hosts an intimidating energy. There are no longer the beautiful smells radiating from fresh laundry; instead, the room holds a nauseating stench powerful enough to turn her insides.

A tear slowly falls down one side of Alice's face. She sees her boys lined up inside the room. And, once again, they're all facing the wall. From out of the darkness come two demonic female figures: a tall woman who is holding baby Hope in her arms and the demonic version of Eve who pushed Alice down the stairs. As they approach Alice they take on human forms. Seeing Jesse and Eve standing before her, Alice cries. Unable to process what she now realises to be the truth, that these two evil entities have been living in her very home, she feels the life draining from her body as she whispers, "Why?"

"Don't take it personally," says Jesse. "You had something we needed. And now you don't. Now we have it." Walking closer to Alice with baby Hope cradled in his arms, Jesse continues, "Now it's time to say goodbye."

Jesse snaps back into demonic form and flashes in front of Alice's face. Screaming out, Alice curls into a ball to try and protect herself. She looks up and sees Eve standing next to Lewis, holding baby Hope in her arms. The children are all mirror images of that horrifying demonic woman, their appearances traumatising and horrific. Devastated, and with her final blast of energy, Alice screams, "No! Please don't take them away from me!"

Laughing, the tall dark woman raises her arms and says, "They were never yours to keep. I am Jezebel. You will never defeat me…"

With a twitch of her head, Jezebel takes full control of Alice's mind. Peering through the gap in her hair, she feeds Alice destructive thoughts. Jezebel whispers under her breath, "It's time, Alice. They're coming and they will pay. It's time to give them what they deserve. She was warned. Your fate is her fault." The thick black substance gushes down her chin as she chants and then suddenly shouts, "Stand!"

Alice lurches to her feet. Blood gushing from her skull, her head flops. Embracing the power that she has over Alice's existence, Jezebel makes her way across the room. As Jezebel leans into Alice's ear, her cold breath touches Alice's skin. No longer in control of her mind, body, or soul, Alice doesn't so much as flinch. Reaching out, Jezebel collects Alice's blood with her finger and begins ingesting this. Suddenly there is a loud squawk. The huge Raven flies into the room and lands on Lewis's shoulder. This intimidating bird begins pecking at the black substance leaving his body. Content, Jezebel leans into Alice's ear once more and says, "Go…"

Alice lifts herself and places one foot in front of the other. As she makes her way across the darkened room, suddenly a bright spotlight appears in the distance. Standing in the background, Jezebel and the newest members of her growing demonic empire all watch as Alice makes her way towards her fate. As she picks up the pace a huge trail of blood follows her. She reaches the spotlight, and in front of Alice is a stool. Without hesitation, she stands on it. Dragging her heavy head, Alice looks up at the thick coarse rope hanging from the ceiling. The rope is dropping down with every second. Eventually it reaches Alice and she holds the noose in her hand. In full control of Alice's movements and thoughts, Jezebel orders her final command: "Do it now."

As soon as the words leave her mouth, Alice places her head inside the noose. It's the seventh of July and the time is now seven. Eve slowly makes her way to Jezebel and hands her baby Hope. Looking at her owner, Eve patiently waits for her command. Sadistic as she is, Jezebel glances at her newest additions. She then releases Alice from the entrapment so she can watch the panic, the fear and the anxiety surging through Alice as her life is being taken from her body. Jezebel wants to watch Alice die. As soon as Jezebel releases Alice, she comes around to reality immediately. "No! No! No! Please, don't do this!" Alice screams.

Getting a thrill from hearing her pleas, Jezebel soon enough nods her head. And, just like that, Eve charges at the stool and kicks it from under Alice's feet. Dangling like a ragdoll, Alice fights to remove the rope from around her neck. Unsuccessful, Alice glances across the room and sees her children. With her last breath she says, "I'm sorry."

As the pressure from the rope serves its purpose, and the last bit of life drains from Alice's body, her arms slump down and hang heavy beside her. Blood begins dripping down her face. Watching, Jezebel and Eve are feeding and gaining strength from the death of Alice.

CHAPTER TWENTY-THREE

It's All Your Fault!

S tanding outside the Parkinsons' house, Matthew says, "I fear we're too late."

He looks up at the sky and sees it is no longer bright. The clouds are an intense shade of grey. It appears as if any minute now a huge earth-shaking storm will take over. The house itself is in complete darkness. Looking up at the sky, Dorothy reaches for the key inside her pocket. Faffing around, she says, "Matthew, don't be silly, they're probably just trying to settle the boys."

Matthew gulps. He would love nothing more than to put his faith and trust in what Dorothy has just said. Unfortunately for her, he has lived this before. His strong gut feeling is telling him something isn't right. After previously ignoring his inner instincts and losing his daughter through his ignorance and stupidity, Matthew now knows to take his gut instinct seriously. He hears it sounding off, the persistent inner voice, like an alarm, screaming at him not to let Dorothy enter the house. If he is right and they are too late, this is going to be far from pleasant.

Now halfway down the path, Dorothy continues to try to find the key. Appearing frustrated, she pulls everything from inside her pocket out and throws it on the ground, eventually finding the keychain containing Alice's keys. She marches to the front door and is about to open it when Matthew grabs her hand. "Dorothy, please, let me go in on my own first. You wait out here and I promise to come and get you if all is okay."

"You can't do that – what if they're in? They'll all have a meltdown if you just start walking around the house."

Confident that there's not a single living soul present inside that house, Matthew says, "Okay, fair point, Dorothy. So, let's ring the doorbell and if no one answers I can go in, but if someone does answer I'll… erm… I'll… I'll use my best Spanish accent and pretend I've got the wrong house. Deal?"

"Fine, deal," Dorothy says, eyeing him with an anxious expression.

While he rings the doorbell, Dorothy jumps to the side of the wall where she can't be seen should one of them answer. Smiling at Dorothy and raising his eyebrows, Matthew says, "No one is coming. *Nada en casa.*"

"Ssshh… someone might come yet," Dorothy says, shutting down his lame broken Spanish joke.

Matthew rings the doorbell once more and waits for a few seconds, then says, "Okay, so there's no one inside this house. Can I have the key now? You're wasting time."

Matthew waits anxiously for Dorothy to hand over the keys. He knows that if he is right, it means he's going to be too late to save his daughter. As she hands him the keys he braces himself and says, "Under no circumstances do you come inside this house." Without a reply, he sternly looks to her and says, "Dorothy, I mean it!"

"Well, what if everything's okay?"

"If everything's okay, I'll shout you. But if I don't, do not enter the house, promise me."

"Okay, okay, I promise."

Not believing a word, Matthew says, "I'll tell you what, why don't you go and sit in the car."

"But how will I hear you shout if everything's okay?"

"I'll come back to the door and wave. Honestly, I think you should just go and sit in the car."

Rolling her eyes, Dorothy does as he asks and makes her way to the car.

Matthew breathes deeply, his heart pounding in his chest. As he unlocks the front door and pushes it open, his nostrils are awakened by a pungent stench. But not just any pungent stench – this smell is all too familiar to Matthew. Covering his nose with his sleeve, Matthew gags as his stomach churns. He takes a step inside the house and slips on a thick substance on the floor. Looking down, he sees a huge puddle of blood. Closing his eyes and trying not to vomit, Matthew lifts his foot out of the dark red smear.

Walking through the hallway, he peers into the day room. It's pitch-black. Closing his eyes and once again bracing himself for what might be hidden in the next room, Matthew heads towards the dining room. A powerful energy is radiating from this section of the house and it's not the welcoming kind. Reaching down the back of his trousers, Matthew grabs his pistol. He holds it in the defence position, his hands shaking. He's nervous about what's on the other side of the closed door.

Breathing deeply, Matthew gathers his strength and pushes the door open. The curtains are pulled tightly shut and the room is overcome by darkness. Reaching for his phone, he puts the torch on as he searches for the light switch on the wall. He finds it and light fills the room. Horrified by what he sees, Matthew runs back the way he came. Bursting out into the garden, he instantly throws up on the grass.

Dorothy flings the car door open and runs towards the house screaming at the top of her voice, "Noooooo!"

Matthew tries to stop her in her tracks, but with the vomit continuing to surge from his stomach he is unsuccessful. He can't stop throwing up. The frantic woman runs straight into the house. Within seconds Matthew hears Dorothy's screams.

"Nooooo! Alice, my baby, Alice."

Hearing her heart-breaking cries, Matthew makes his way back inside the house. Running into the dining room, Matthew grabs Dorothy and attempts to pull her out of the house. Like a deadweight, Dorothy falls to the floor. At the top of her voice she cries, "Why God, why? My baby. My beautiful baby girl."

Crying silently as he holds Dorothy in his arms, Matthew looks across at what has disturbed them both so much. Swinging from a rope is Alice Parkinson. Her eyes are bulging from their sockets and a pool of blood is on the ground beneath her. On the wall, smeared with this thick red bloody substance, are the words " *You were warned, her fate is your fault*".

Broken, Dorothy shoots up off the ground and rushes towards Alice. Grabbing her daughter, she's frantically attempts to remove the rope from round her neck. Screaming, she says, "Matthew, help me. We might not be too late, we can still save her. Help me get her down."

Kneeling on the floor, aware there's no undoing what has been done, Matthew is holding his head in his hands. Struggling with the bodyweight of her daughter, Dorothy screams once more, "Matthew, help me!"

Matthew stands and makes his way to Dorothy, but instead of helping her get Alice down, he attempts to pull her out of the room. Resisting, Dorothy reaches out for her daughter as she screams at the top of her voice, "Let go of me. Alice... Alice... I'm sorry!"

Not wanting to leave Dorothy alone with her deceased daughter, Matthew says, "Dorothy, it's okay, I'm here, shhh... I'm so sorry."

"Why was she even here?" Dorothy questions as she's crying. "Matthew she should have been at the hospital. Why Alice? Why...?"

Inconsolable, Dorothy tucks herself into Matthew's arms. He says nothing as he holds her tightly. Kissing her on the head, as the time passes, he says, "Dorothy, I'm going to search upstairs. I think you should go and sit back inside the car."

Dorothy pushes herself out of Matthew's arms and screams at the top of her voice, "You sick bastard, where are you? Come on, take me as well."

She gets up and runs up the stairs, seemingly ready to tackle the evil that has ruined her life. Following her with his pistol in his hand, Matthew runs up the staircase. They search every room and discover that the house is empty. They're too late. The beds are all neatly made and there isn't a child in sight.

Suddenly, Matthew and Dorothy hear a male voice shout, "Hello?" It's coming from downstairs.

Matthew makes his way to the top of the staircase and yells, "Who's that?"

"Is that Matthew?"

Now even more concerned, Matthew runs down the stairs and Dorothy's quick to follow. When he gets halfway down, Matthew sees a smartly dressed man and woman standing in the doorway. They each have their noses covered and are desperately attempting to shield themselves from the stench that's circulating. Their faces look familiar. Confused, Matthew says, "Do I know you?"

"Yes, Matthew I'm DCS Terry and this is my colleague DC Flores. We've been following you for some time. Can we ask what's going on in here?"

"Wait a minute – you've been following me? What gives you the right to do that?"

"You're the Police?" Dorothy cuts in.

DC Flores replies, "Yes, is everything okay?"

"No! My daughter's dead in that room and my grandchildren have been kidnapped. Someone needs to help me!"

Seemingly mystified at her words, DCS Terry looks to his colleague.

"Sir, we need to call this in," DC Flores says.

"Sorry, where's your daughter?" DCS Terry says to Dorothy.

Hysterical, she points to the dining room.

"Okay, you stay here. I'm going to have a look with my colleague."

Making their way across to the room, DCS Terry and DC Flores struggle to hold down their vomit. The stench circulating is taking over. Slipping and losing his footing, DCS Terry looks to the ground. He sees a thick black substance smeared across the floor.

Looking to her colleague, DC Flores says, "Sir, you okay?"

"Yeah, Flores, I'm good. What is this on the floor?"

She sees the thick black substance and follows the tainted trail with her eyes. "I don't know, sir, but it's taking us into that room."

They cautiously make their way to the dining room. As they enter, the stench becomes unbearable. Burying their noses into the sleeves on their jackets, DCS Terry and DC Flores try not to vomit when they see a woman hanging from the ceiling. DC Flores retches, turning her back on the swinging corpse. Making his way towards the deceased body, DCS Terry begins calling Chief Inspector Lamont.

As the phone rings, suddenly he sees a twitch come from the fingers of the deceased body. He concentrates, getting closer and closer, when suddenly the female body springs to life and throws herself at DCS Terry and attempts to grab him. Screaming, both he and DC Flores run out of the house and into the garden.

When the two detectives emerge, Matthew and Dorothy run into the dining room. Seeing nothing but Alice swinging from the ceiling, once again Dorothy breaks down. Sobbing, this broken woman is on her knees. Suddenly both Matthew and Dorothy hear DCS Terry say, "Excuse me, you can't go in there. Oi, are you listening to me?"

Hearing a familiar voice, Dorothy looks up.

Responding to DCS Terry this male says, "Don't tell me I can't go in here. Alice?"

Walking out of the room, Dorothy can't believe what she's seeing. Wiping her puffy eyes, she's convinced she's seeing things. Staring at her, the man says, "Dorothy, where's Alice and the children? What's going on? Who are all these people?"

Gobsmacked, her eyes are pinned open wide. In disbelief Dorothy says, "Phil?"

Even though he isn't dressed in his usual smart, cool, surfer dude attire, there's no getting away from the fact that this is Phil Parkinson standing in the doorway. With his full beard and scruffy appearance, Phil is looking at Dorothy with tears in his eyes and his hand over his nose. As Dorothy remains silent, he appears more and more alarmed by the second.

"Dorothy, please, where are Alice and the boys?"

Still, Dorothy says nothing as the tears fall down her motionless face. Putting his head down, Matthew whispers, "I'm sorry, we were too late."

"Too late... too late for what?" As the silence continues Phil once again raises his voice, "Will someone give me answers. What is going on?"

Keeping his head down, Matthew says, "We couldn't save them."

"Save them?" Seeming confused he says, "I'm sorry, mate, but who the fuck are you? And what's that smell?" Looking to his mother-in-law Phil continues, "Dorothy, I need you to tell me what's happened."

Crying her eyes out she says, "Tell you what's happened? You're supposed to be dead. Why and how are you even here? None of this would have happened if you were here and hadn't abandoned them leaving them to fend for themselves. Where the fuck have you been, Phil?"

Trying to dodge the swinging fists, Phil grabs Dorothy to restrain her as he says, "Dorothy, please calm down. I had to do it. I had to do it for the family. We can talk about that later, please just tell me where they are."

Crying and throwing herself to the floor Dorothy points to the dining room and says, "She's in there."

Pushing past Matthew, Phil runs into the dining room. Within seconds he screams, "Nooooo!"

Standing in the garden DCS Terry is on the phone to Chief Inspector Lamont. He's trying to explain what's currently happening. DC Flores is consoling Dorothy in the doorway and Matthew has made his way back into the dining room. Struggling, Phil is trying to get his precious wife down from the swinging rope. Helping, Matthew grabs her legs so that Phil can release her from the rope. Lying her on the ground, a mess, Phil can't stop crying as he cradles his deceased wife.

The house has been cordoned off with police tape and the streets have been taken over by multiple ambulances and police cars with flashing lights. Government officials are swarming all over Shayfield Street. Sat in the back of an ambulance, Dorothy is howling as her heart breaks into a million pieces. Rocking back and forth, she's screaming, "Why God, my baby, why my baby? Please give her back... please, not my baby... I have nothing."

Sitting on the kerb outside the house with his head in his hands, Phil's struggling to piece together the realities before him. Matthew sits down next to Phil. "Sorry, pal," he says.

"Sorry for what? Did you do this?!"

"No, no! Good Lord no!" Holding his hands up Matthew continues, "I lost my wife and daughter to this same sick individual."

"So what are you sorry for?"

"I'm sorry I didn't piece it together sooner. I might have been able to stop her."

"Stop who? Where are they? Do you know where they are?"

"God no – I've been trying to find my daughter for almost a year now." Matthew can't hold back any longer. "I'm sorry, but Dorothy said you were dead. She said you killed yourself."

Hanging his head with shame, tears uncontrollably welling in his eyes, Phil tells the truth. "I faked my own death. I was in too much debt and was worth more dead than alive. I couldn't have Alice for a second believe that I was still living, she'd go to prison and I wasn't having that..."

"Wait, so what did you think – you could just pop up one day?"

"Yeah – I don't know, my head was in bits and all I could think about was the brand-new baby girl that was going to grow up with nothing. I was sick of the debt, the threats, the constant chasing, so I decided the only way it would all go away was if I did."

"I... I mean... how did you even... I-I'm sorry, I'm just so confused."

"Believe me, I'm so ashamed. I'm a coward, I know. For months I've been across the road. You see that derelict building there?"

"Yes."

"I've been keeping my eye on them all this time. When I saw Alice with a new man and a daughter it just seemed impossible to come clean. The lie got too deep."

"So what, you just let your family believe you were dead, your children grow up without a father, your wife live without a husband?"

But before Phil can answer the question, Dorothy appears from nowhere and hits him over the back of the head with her fist. She screams at him, "You bastard, you should be dead, not her. You should have been taken, not her and my kids. You bastard. You better go and kill yourself for real." The police come over and restrain Dorothy. Screaming one final time she spits at him and shouts, "I'm going to kill you."

Phil is crying his eyes out. "She's right. Dorothy's right. I should be the one that's dead. I left my family broken, vulnerable and weak for the sake of money, debt and pride."

With the private ambulance outside ready to transport the deceased's body, the coroner begins wheeling the trolley which is carrying Alice out of the house. They've placed her inside a zipped black bag in order to conceal her lifeless corpse, which was already turning blue. Seeing the trolley, Phil runs over. Throwing himself on top of the body bag he cries out, "I'm so sorry. Her name is Help. Our daughter's name is Help. Hope is HELP – Hope Ella Lia Parkinson. I thought one day you would work this out. I thought you'd find my notes in the house and come to me." As the tears stream from his eyes and fall rapidly off his face, Phil cries his final words to his wife, "I am so sorry, my queen, I'm coming for you."

Reaching over to Phil, Matthew pulls him away. Holding this broken man's face in his hands and looking him directly in the eye, Matthew says, "I will find her. She will pay for this. I will get our children back. But right now, you need to man up, you need to change, you need to stop being a coward by running away at the first hurdle."

Phil looks back a Matthew, his face is swollen. Sobbing, he replies, "We will find her, and when we do, I'm going to kill the bitch by pulling her fucking heart out with my bare hands."

The two broken men stare at one another intently. They're oblivious to the commotion surrounding them. They're ready to team up and kill the demonic entity who has ruined their lives and claim back what's left of their families. But the question is, who will win control of their souls...?

Will Matthew and Phil work out the tainted trail before them? Or will Jezebel and Eve cunningly continue to build their empire and take control of not only the world, but the universe and all that lies within? And so, just like that, the hunt continues...

ABOUT THE AUTHOR

 A.L. Frances is a thirty-two-year-old, British Author.

The Broken II – Tainted Trail is the second book of a four-part series and marks A.L. Frances' debut in literary fiction.

Born in Wythenshawe, South Manchester, she is the product of a broken home. Her formal education was cut short before she could gain any qualifications and she became a mother to three children by the time she was just twenty years old. At twenty-one A.L. Frances suddenly finds herself cast in the role of a single parent, destined to repeat the cycle of her own difficult upbringing.

Determined to give her children a better start in life, she moved to the countryside village of Hollingworth, and eventually settled into a career in law. It was during this transition that she found herself on a journey of self-discovery. Attending multiple mindset enhancing seminars in England, America and Canada, she was exposed to the tutelage of inspirational speakers such as Bob Proctor, Tony Robbins, and Mel Robbins among others. A.L. Frances was eventually introduced to Peggy McColl, a New York Times Best Selling Author. Standing on the stage, Peggy said the words that would inspire her into action. Peggy said, "Everyone has a book in them." as she pointed into the crowd. It was at this point that A.L. Frances fell in love with the idea of writing her own book and telling her own story; one that would address one of her biggest fears: the vulnerabilities of broken homes.

At the age of twenty-nine, A.L. Frances decided it was time to start the next chapter of her life.

What follows is the continuation of her journey…